I0676891

MIRACULUM

By :

Suzanna
Terrell

**A DEMON, IN
THERAPY!**

"MIRACULUM"

Fiction. A Novel By:

Suzanna Marie Terrell

©Copyright 2012© By Suzanna Terrell

©Copyright 2013© By Suzanna Terrell

Cover Page Art Design By: …Suzanna Terrell & Star Melody Terrell

Many thanks to my daughter, Star Melody, for helping with both typing & the cover page. I Love You Star!

Suzanna Terrell is also Author of the True Story:

a) **"COMFORT SOUP FOR THE MIND"**

b) **"HANDBOOK FOR THE DEAD,**

THE LIVING DEAD, AND THOSE WHO OCCASSIONALLY WISHED THEY WERE DEAD" Which can be found at: www.createspace.com/3393541 & www.amazon.com

Suzanna Terrell is Author of: **HEALING FROM : TRAUMA [CD #1] and [CD # 2]** -- Includes Healing From Severe Post Traumatic Stress

The Most POWERFUL Healing TECHNIQUES For:

Divorce, Severe Post Traumatic Stress Disorder, Kidnapping, Rape, Abuse, Injustice, Loss of a Loved-One, Harm or Loss of a Child, and other traumatic events.
These CD's can be found at: [CD #1] www.createspace.com/2018745 [CD #2] createspace.com/2023259 And also at: www.amazon.com

ONE

Dr. Roberts could not get the man to talk about his body modifications! Usually when she would ask him about it he would snort puffs of air from his nose, fling his hands into the ethers and with a roll of his eyes stomp out of the office without saying a word. He wouldn't tell her his name!

With stoic patience Dr. Roberts would immerse herself in pithy cool forbearance with a tolerably restful composure to lurch forth with stolid fortitude the stony tramples this wondering outlander strangled back in choking indignation the telltale temerity of his haunting tormented troubles. Sometimes when Dr. Roberts asked about his body modifications the man would bend his head and pull at his horns to insist that they were real! As absurd as this was the Doctor felt with aching sympathy how his disturbed rowel showed his predicament of inflamed annoyance; his agitation to retreat into a less infested world of whimsical dreamy fantasy. To insist that his horns were real! So sad indeed. Dr. Roberts would ask him how he felt when they put the implants under his skull; if he had to unscrew his horns and take them off to sleep at night. How did he get his skin that color—was it all tattooed?

Dr. Roberts charged the man hardly anything at all since he made his money making 'muscle-man' poses whilst other people put money in a hat he found when he was in New York City's central park. He said he slept on top of building roofs but that it wasn't really sleep, it was more like a quiet meditative floatiness. The tattooed man had several times pounded his back, turning as if to show her that once upon a time he had wings; that all of his kin could deliberate a flourish of will and with a rainbow of colored feathers between them they could fly, hunt; but that somehow his ability to induce his wispy wingspan had slowed over time, eventually stopping all together. One time after one such rant from the hungry-eyed man the Doctor had him sit cross-legged, down on the floor with her, to do some true therapy. He would feel his feeling of fear and give it a symbol then let it go and see it with the symbol he assigned outside of himself; then he would feel happiness with a symbol he gave it then set it aside, next he was instructed to feel nothing with equally assigned symbol, until he could give and take away each feeling/symbol to lastly assign a new symbol of *control*. During this session a glimmering raven-like feather had floated down as if it had appeared mystic all on its own from the ceiling. The feather landed from its waft, onto the floor, where it lay between them. He insisted this was a sign, probably from one of his family he said, that it was proof he did indeed once have wings. Dr. Roberts had no recourse but to admit she had no idea where on earth the feather came from. This did nothing to aid her in grabbing his mind and pulling it back to reality! He changed the subject when she broached his past; primarily the man wanted to talk about conscientious subjects. A man of spirited philosophical phlegmatic bounce it seemed to sooth like a salve the bodacious seething abscess that inflamed his brazen wounded soul when he pontificated the phantasmic orchestra of the cosmos. They would often spend the entire hour in zipping moments where he asked about existence; he paced and talked about humanity; the universe. He pondered good and evil.

Mostly the man talked about his 'Home-Planet'; he was pressingly emphatic that he wanted to tell the Doctor his story. Yet this man would cross his large arms to stare with frustration, shaking his head from side to side when Dr. Roberts implored him to tell her his story, so that they spent the entire hour in silence, while she occasionally interrupted the quiet with statements like, "I'm ready. I'm listening."

Once, she had caught him just before he walked out the door destitute of convictional devotion and dejected by the writhing boil in his soul that seemed to moor the devouring of his mind like a delicacy, and she said, "Please! Let me Help you! Tell me your story! I am listening!"

He had looked at her while holding the door half open from the side-glance of his sad mournful eyes, speaking low and temberous he said, "It's *too* horrible. It will scare you."

"But I want you to show me the horrible. I want you to tell me. If we can bravely face what is most horrible then we can let go of our horror and at last move forward. We see the horror for what it was; and then we move forward, see? And things get better. *Be brave!*" The man had simply shaken his head again. He left the office slamming the door like a quaking ache of anger behind him.

His diagnosis would not be easy considering the disingenuous disheartening discord with which he argued his cryptic flood of philosophical and natural debacle debate of the ebbing flowing human mind, the appeasing vivacious ranting grumble labyrinth of science. To disentangle the man's snug demarcation, pulling the doxy of truth into lightsome freedom might remove his soul's snare to provide him the prerogative of being himself, understand his life; give to him carte blanche the liberating immunity of an amicable existence without remedy of resorting to a final climax of at least too many medications. Dr. Roberts felt the need to fastidiously and methodically proceed with a modus operandi of no medications for now so that with a clear mind the man might conscientiously mine his intelligence towards a fundamental acceptance of himself and a migratory release of whatever events or horrors were his past.

Thus Doctor Roberts would not give up on this strange man. If ever a man needed help, this particular circus man needed it the most. She was dedicated; defalcation was not an option in her devotion to an individual in need no matter how partisan. She was determined and predisposed to fervid faithful succours of comfort. *She wanted to help.* So today Dr. Roberts had a plan.

A little psychological trickery on her part!

Dr. Roberts was old, an antiqued perennial pomegranate sweetly ripened wise; prominently pleated with wrinkles, and imposed to irascible liver-spots which she belligerently rucked with fade-cream to no avail. Winters stage of age had revolved the reflection of every strand of her hair to the snowy white swathed by the ravages of time. With an encouraged celestial strength of heart that was deeply sincere she felt she could finally get the man to speak and tell his story; to discuss his body modifications, his feelings.

He was always talking about his 'Home-Planet', so she derived the idea that today she would talk about her own story. She would employ her empirical warm congeniality and understanding to entrench her insight with inspired invention to draw out the better welfare of the man. Dr. Roberts would implore the circus man's inner spirit to reach for healing by using her empathy, intuition and imagination.

Thus when the man came in this sunny day to sit upon the couch in her office, she said: "Today I will tell you *my* story. I will begin how I see it, how I feel it, how it seems to me *my* Home-Planet would be." The man leaned forward arching one eyebrow in obvious undisguised curiosity. That was a good sign. He placed his elbows on his knees, squinted his eyes at the doctor.

So Dr. Roberts pulled her computer sideways where she could type but still see the man. As a psychiatrist of good heart, Dr. Roberts pulled up an empty page document on her computer. As she typed she spoke her written words out loud: "I use the words 'Home-Planet because to simply say "Home" is too abstract. On my Home-Planet I am the Mother-Angel; I am the Observer. Of this particular type of Angel, there are only two of us: Observers. There is the Mother, and there is the Father. I am the Mother. I perform a very important service for the beings on my planet…I am the Observer, ..and where would a rock-star be without an observer? Where would a famous actor or actress be without someone to observe them, love them, and adore them? Mother-Angel; Father-Angel."

"I miss the Father whom is there as I am for him, so that we might observe each other…for on my Home-Planet even an Observer needs an Observer. And the Father and I are the Admiring, Unconditionally Loving, Observers of all the Beings and Beauty and Existence of our Home."

"You're interrupting me." Calm, deep-dark enchanting, beautiful voice purring, rumbling the words.

"Pardon?" Dr. Roberts looked up at the man. Turning her swiveling desk-chair around with her toes she faced him directly. She had been typing on the computer and speaking her writing out loud when the man spoke. It was another good sign. Perhaps this was the moment of revelation by which come dew or storm she must harbor her stirring excitement to maintain composure, stay calm, be for this patient an alleviating balm. Giving him her full attention, she squinted her eyes with her heart full of true hope. "But you said we should start from the beginning", said Dr. Roberts hoping to keep the man talking.

"Yes." He returned his answer to her in that lulling deep resonance of voice. "But I said I wanted to tell *my* story. You said I could." He was emotionless yet with firm calm in his voice both at the same moment.

Always the counselor at such times as this when she desired to give her full listening attention to another! The Doctor nodded her head in the affirmative. "Go ahead", she encouraged, "I'm listening."

"Well so far your beginning with *your* story."

"Yes", she was trying to think fast, "I thought that since your story and my story collide in this office, then the obvious start...", she paused, "...would be...to start at the beginning. So I... I..." She struggled.

"*Your* beginning."

"How so?" Rubbing her chin out of reflex, squinting her eyes to focus in on his words, she struggled with her hopes to keep him talking. "I don't understand", said Dr. Roberts thoughtfully. Her right-hand palm raised up toward the ceiling as she stretched then rested her elbow upon the chair's arm-rest. He was still and quiet so she said, "I don't see how there's any difference; any separation...isn't it true that your story and my story intertwine here in my office…and isn't that a beginning?" 'Keep talking. Please keep talking!'—she silently willed to the man with all her heart. Dr. Robert's rubbed her chin again, trying to think of what to say. "Wouldn't the beginning of my story be the very interlude to the entrance of *your* story?"

He placed his large raw fingers upon his own chin turning his face to the left, away from her gaze. Seconds ticked on the clock. "As you know", he began and breathed through his nostrils several times flaring them, "As you *should* know, my people heard that when our world was created that 'It was Good.'" His face jerked towards her; he met her eyes with a teary pain and sorrow that nevertheless expected the whole room and all that one can see to come to *him*. He continued speaking. "We thought *we* were the 'Good' ones! We thought *we* were the only blessed. Then many of my kind came here to this earth, this damnation, and all of us were outraged to be called 'evil'. Outraged to have your kind systematically saying we should go back to 'hell'. To hell! We do not come from hell!" Leaning forward with his elbows on his parted knees, he clasped his hands together in interlaced fingers that grew red-knuckled with his intensity of emotion. "We are of one mind, my people. Yet we inhabit our own gracious bodies. Separate bodies. Yet a shared mind."

"Yes. I know…umm…" It was working! Her plan was working! Dr. Roberts was so excited she wanted to jump up and do a happy-joy dance. Yet of course such a thing would be inappropriately absurd; so she contained her excitement by sipping from the bottle of water she kept on her desk. Her mouth parted to draw in a breath. "So you feel so much strongly for one another. You love each other with a deepness and connection that the 'Good'

could not even begin to understand."
Eyes softening, she parted her lips then
gently pressed them into a warm lift at
the corners that was almost like a smile.
"But evil must not hurt 'good'. 'Good'
really does exist. And good feels the
pain much worse than you…" Tilting
her head to the right in slight deferment,
"And while I know that 'good' have their
own conscious minds…" She paused to
get her words straight; to keep him
telling his story *"Your* kind have a sort
of integral psychic connection
consciously."

"We are of one mind!!" He was
trying to stay calm but the urgent passion
in his voice belied him. "We are many!"

"Like a legion?" She gave herself
those closed lips to have a soft near smile
again.

"Don't bring the Bible into this." He
looked away and snorted a shot of air
from his nostrils.

"Shall I pick another religion?" Dr. Roberts softly giggled.

"Don't be funny." Yet his deep voice was velvety soft as he smiled despite himself.

"But I am funny." Her eyes lit up. "Now that's something I should let *you* know about me. Deep inside I have a very good sense of humor." Great were her hopes to sooth and relax away any of his dungeonous deep anxieties so that he might continue to converse.

He looked at Dr. Roberts giving a tisking smirkish grin. Eyes roving about the room all at once the man took in the decoration of the office. She too felt compelled to glance around the room. Light salmon-pink walls, with a dark blue ceiling. Just above the furniture some of her own paintings she had hung upon the walls; mainly portraits in vivid color excepting the painting of 'death' with a skeleton companion cat beside the grim reaper. Serenely set were a vine of cream swirls amidst gentle blues that made the border—it was about five inches deep, nearly touching the ceiling. The wall border had an appealing calming affect. In the corner stood Dr. Roberts bookcase, made of wood, tall, and created precisely to look like a boat. A boat standing up with it's slim pointy top facing upwards, its body full of books on ancient looking wood boards sufficing as shelves. They both breathed while glancing about the room, he and the doctor, in this extended unassuming silence.

At once he stood to his feet. The doctor was suddenly frightened that he would leave. He wrung his bulging hands together while he looked up to the ceiling. "The Lord my God has many kingdoms!", the doctor said urgently and desperately.

"*Many Worlds*!" He shouted this as his eyes flared with a glassy light for a moment when he stared at Dr. Roberts.

"Same thing!"

"Will you stop that!?"

"Am I annoying you?"

"*It's my God too*!" He pulled his tight fists on either side of him in the air and squeezed the muscles of his arms tight. "*My* God too! *My* universal intelligence! *My* creator!" His voice suddenly roared with what seemed to be anger. His body muscles tight with rage. While he did this his eyes seemed to pull all of the light of the room in towards himself. Raising his arms high in a tense aggressive inner-horror, his voice rumbled like a roll of thunder: "*My* God too!!"

Instantly he realized his digression, pulling his arms to his chest, he wrapped his hands together again bringing them to rest at his stomach.

Placing her eyes in a squinted lock upon one spot on the floor so that she might keep a deeper inner-focus she breathed in, nodding her head. "Now", she said thoughtfully, for they had dealt with loud expressiveness like this sort of roaring before. Setting her elbows upon her office chair armrests again, Dr. Roberts lifted her hands before herself with open hands then placed her fingertips to touch lightly against one another. Looking up at him the doctor opened her mouth to speak but was struck motionless mute when she saw his face.

He was biting one side of his bottom lip, his eyes had the wetness and wide-opened look of a worry that did not suck in the light of the room but instead projected that light outwards so that he might take in the looks of *her*...so that he might *see* her.

"I know", he spoke softly. For he had to be gentle with her. He had to be tender. She was not like him.

Dr. Roberts began sweetly: "You can have a strong passionate feeling and when you are with your like-kind, your soul family from Home…that can and does feel the same passion, your same strength, then it is okay." Dr. Roberts said this while tilting her head and keeping her expression compassionate. "But for *my* kind…well, it only scares me."

"Yes." He conceded. His voice was forcefully softly lowered. "Your Kind. And my Kind. And all the souls and kingdoms, and everything in between, like a spectrum of lights of many colors from one side to the other." He let out an exasperated breath then pressed his lips together. Breathing in through his nostrils he purred with his voice, "I'm *trying*."

It seemed Dr. Roberts wanted to say something at that moment, but as she went to speak her mind was filled with a heavy pull of color and familiarity--like a memory that was trying to break through. She was rendered unable to say any response at all for the moment. There was a pressure in her consciousness of blurry images pressing against her skull; what seemed like a memory she knew with all her heart and soul but could not yet see.

He got down on his knees in front of her, a burning painful unconditional love that she could feel as a palpable energy poured forth from his soul for her. For the doctor. Instinctively, like a mother to her newborn, Dr. Roberts placed her hand upon his face feeling his leathery warm skin against her palm. His skin was thick as buffalo hide and red-orange-brown like a sunset color. She knew he looked the way he did because he wanted too. He could have had any modified tattooed appearance he chose. (This was so much more true than she ever actually suspected.)

Yet he knew he had chosen the look, shape, color and huge, tall, wide, immensity of body because it was all a part of what made him say, "Yes. *Oh yes*; this is *me*."

His brow was wide, but his eyes looked human. Except for the color. The color of his eyes were a magnetizing, shining, very-light (in fact almost clear) color of yellow. The doctor thought they were contact lenses. Her right-hand fingertips rolled almost imperceptibly from the lobe of his ear, across the tip top of his ear. Then very barely touching, like a light breath of outdoor breeze her fingertips traced past the top of his ear to the edge of his temple, to the bottom of his horn. Both horns on his head were thick, solid, hard, swirling. Her fingertips traced his dark sunset colored hide in an 's' that lifted up into a thinner curled tip at the top of the horn. He bowed his head and closed his eyes.

Placing her palm to rest against the back of his leathery hairless head, she said, "Yes. It is your *story*. You asked me to hear *your* story." Retracting her hand, placing it to rest in her lap, she watched as he slowly lifted his face upward towards her; gazing with pain into the retina of her own eyes. "What was it you wanted to say?"—the doctor asked.

He pressed his lips together, then spoke with forceful sorrow:

"I Am Miraculum."

TWO

       Miraculum was Home, that was *his* Heaven; *his* planet. This is where his story started. He marched about this day with his iridescent raven wings of six feet across spun out behind him like a comforting cape. Walking around the big long pale-oak table that was set outside in the open colored aura of soft breezy air, he grinned from ear to ear. He scratched his horns, cut a joke, everyone standing or sitting about the table laughed with drunken glee.

The sky was a pale green with swaths of darker green; blue-aqua smeared across it's majesty here and there. The clouds were puffs that never moved; of frothy white; they cast no shadow.

Often every one of them would envelope the air awash with their varied-colored wide feathered flanks flapping ginger from the articulated rachis column of their gangling backs, at mere will, in order to assist the vivacious fun of leaping and flying ahead when in barbarian pursuit of their kill. This whop of wings and fastidious display of skill made the hunt more thrilling. They could chase and surround their prey. The meal were of various creatures that weren't even real, that set about no sounds of fear or squeals of concern when hunted then seized with pithy causatum, but were there just to magically reappear and give a good emotionless, expressionless, chase so that they may be caught and all whom were pursuing could tear them apart. These creatures weren't real at all but a set program, like a 4D projection from some massive computer as it were for lack of any better description, as one could tell by their lack of expression or emotion;

by the fact that once they had been torn
apart in a massive messy bloody splash
these 'background' unreal creatures
would vanish. That which they chose not
to take back to the bar-b-q and grill
would simply sparkle and disappear. So
that Miraculum and his friends could
give a charming, sweating, marathon race
chase down the buffalo-sized elk-shaped
creature with beautiful smooth snake-like
skin; give it a good pounce and sports-
like wrestle. Then tear it apart with
blood-drops the size of dinner plates
floating as if slowly suspended in air—
tearing off a leg or a head or whatever
part they fancied, to shout and jump with
exhilarated joy. Then before their eyes
the heavenly hologram would clean up
it's own mess. All blood and bones and
fur or scales would simply sparkle like
bursts of tiny sunlight shining from it,
and completely disappear. Moon-washed
dematerialized fading specters.

They would be left with whatever arm, leg, foot or eyeball that they wanted sitting delightfully in their hands. They would take these trophies back and slap them on the grill to cook them. Some in their clan; Miraculum's family, were quite smart about mixing various fungi, herbs, and potions, to put on the meat as it cooked in a magnanimous waft of luscious smells. Not a one of them actually needed to eat in order to survive. It was simply tasty; and fun.

"Survival" was not even a word that was needed. None of them needed to "survive". Life was an eternal lush of games and camaraderie. There was no such emotion as "boredom" for them to even feel. Such a thing as boredom wasn't even programmed into their physical existence.

Licentious liberation from imbecilic compendium of gormandizing edibles was an ebullience of pure freedom! They could eat all they wanted, but never be required to pee or poo or even fart, because the "food" would simply sparkle and disappear from existence the moment they swallowed it. It was an illusion they savored nevertheless. Harmonic comestibles converged a happy festivity!

Daft cockamamie horseplay led to ludicrous jolly adventures of zany days spent clowning gastronome and excrescence induced hilarity. Being a rowdy crowd with boisterously lurid humor, they would often "create" a pee or poo or fart which would not sparkle or disappear until they wanted it too. This was a source of great laughter, and many pranks. Exuberant tomfoolery unearthed the silliness of sincere hearted fun and humor.

Now it shouldn't be thought that only evil holds the full rights to fart jokes. Vellecating a jolly jest had ecstatic dram that chinkles concourse mirth. There are some Kingdoms (or Homes, Heavens, Universes, Home-planets, whatever you want to call it) that are on the other side of the spectrum and are very, very good, and in fact enjoy a nice fart joke themselves... especially gnomes and flower-fairies. Gnomes and flower-fairies are very 'Good' and are especially keen on an auspicious fart joke! The only difference is: flower-fairies can make fart jokes glittery and shiny; a most favored talent. Crafty, skillful, endowment of expertise charm was daringly spirited in the volage boon of benevolent contribution via exploding excreta and gastrulation.

Miraculum stood about the long table with his friends surrounded, as he absent-mindedly picked the inside of his fingernail with the tip of his right horn that protruded delightfully from his head. He was grinning like a mad-cat, so full of deep love and joy to be with his friends.

"Come, Miraculum!"—"Sit at the table!", said Tobias with a boisterous glee. Tobias was hairy from head to toe

with long auburn fur, he was rather fond
of wearing fine silk suits with jackets that
had long black tails down the back of the
jacket's rococo fabric. His face wasn't
hairy at all however, in fact he had a
rather handsome face in his almost
auburn colored skin. To Tobias's
chagrin he would often wake from a nap
to find his friends laughing and giggling
ridiculously only to discover they had put
braids in his hair with giant stinging bees
stuck into the braids! Tobias's fingers
would get stung repeatedly as he ran
about happily screaming like an idiot
trying to pull out the braids and the giant
bees.

Now it should be noted here that if
you come from the spectrum of, say, the
very, very good, your Heaven or Home-
Planet does not experience pain; pain
simply does not exist. Nor in a 'very
good' Home are there any flies or
mosquitoes or worms or bugs or
stinging-things. Nor in such good

Kingdoms are there anything which bite or hurt you; they simply don't exist. Oh now in a very good heaven they do have some bugs, but they are very large and beautiful and love to have conversations. Embellished insectum marauders spouting masterful prose; perhaps exclusively to their own delight, despite their insistence of words found multifariously rich. Sometimes everyone else up and goes, leaving the massive gorgeous bugs to effluvia the beauty of their pontifications simply amongst themselves; so that all who left find themselves pondering: 'How can anyone possibly chit-chat so much?'

In a very evil heaven there are bugs and animals which exist there of their own right. One never hunts these creatures, but one might gather a great party together to go poke and tease these creatures whom themselves love the challenge. Thaumaturgic creatures whom one treasures all intriguing billet-doux flirtation. If, for example, Miraculum and his friends were having great fun poking and teasing, say, one of the crocodiles, it's entirely possible one of the party would get their foot chomped off by the crocodile who would chew the foot very, very slowly with satisfaction. This brings us to another incredibly important thing to exude upon for remembrance. It must be pointed out that Beings who are evil and live an evil heaven do not feel pain as a 'human' on earth might feel pain. For those in an evil Home-Planet like Miraculum's, pain has a small bit of an 'ow' to it but then it feels pleasurable… like a hundred-thousand pleasurable tingles floating up from their toes to their head and back down again. They also regenerate; like a salamander on earth might have it's tail cut off then the tail grows back again. Only as one might have guessed by now, Miraculum and his kind can regenerate a body part such as a foot so quickly that it is absolutely brilliant!

"Come sit!"—commanded Tobias to Miraculum.

Miraculum, who hardly ever wore a shirt because he liked to show off his reddish skin with tight taught muscles, beat his chest smiling with deep happiness. Miraculum and his kind did not think of themselves as evil, nor did they think of their heaven home-planet as 'Hell'. They had been told their world was good when it was made thus they took this statement to a deeper level and believed it with all their hearts. They had heard rumors, tales, about the 'Ones' who called themselves 'Good' and thought of Miraculum and his kind, *and* their worlds as 'evil'...this angered them completely!

Miraculum beat his chest again saying in a deep roaring voice, "Yes! Let us all sit Brethren! Brethren! Let us all feast!" With this said, Miraculum pulled out a chair and sat down.

Grolin the giant was standing beside the bar-b-q grill wearing only what could be described as looking like tight red spandex underwear; (which he was teased about endlessly.) 'He just liked the color red; so there!' Everyone sat about the table as Grolin grabbed pieces of darkened meat, picking the hot meat up with his bare hands he tossed this grub skillfully to land upon the table directly in front of each person seated.

Suddenly Ramley stood up from the table smiling, grabbed his hatchet out of the leather holster he wore around his waist, and just as Barlee who sat on the other side of the table reached for his piece of meat, Ramley swung his hatchet down to perfectly cut off Barlee's arm! Blood splattered and floated into the air then began to audibly *purr* out crimson in a thick pool of blood across the table. Everyone, including Barlee, laughed and laughed. Roared in fact with great heaps of hearty laughter. Barlee shouted 'ow!'

Then he shuddered from the tingle of it. Barlee's hand and arm began regenerating immediately so that he had a new one. The blood spatter began to sparkle and disappear from the air. The thick pool of blood on the table began to sparkle and disappear. Yet just as the severed arm began to sparkle and disappear, Ramley snatched it up, where it instantly stopped sparkling to become solid again. Ramley pulled off the left-over bit of leather sleeve that was upon the arm when chopped off; he tossed the leather bit to the ground where it promptly disappeared. "Here!"— shouted Ramley to Grolin. Ramley threw the arm to Grolin, whereby it missed Grolin's hands completely yet landed with a plop perfectly upon the grill. The arm with hand still attached began to bar-b-q and brown up nicely.

Laughter trickled into giggles and harrumphs until in a pause of silence Sana shoved her elbow into Gabirr's ribs speaking onward despite his responsive 'Hey, ouch!' "I was walking alone, communing with nature, when my gruesome lot of supposed friends here ruined it!" (Many groaned. "She's always complaining about something," said Aapep.) "Oh I heard that!"—grieved Sana with a grin whereby she then picked up a silver fork and throwing it at Aapep watched it bounce off of his schnozzle to tinkle with a pretty plink upon the table. "Anyway, as I was saying before so rudely interrupted by you apes," Sana continued, "I was communing with nature when Betsura, Jenday, and Yong-Sun-Sook caused me to crap half out of my sandals by making loud outrageous noises!"

"What did they do?"—asked Sekhet scratching the entrance of her nose with her long blue fingernail—"say 'Boo'!?" Everyone at the long table grumbled with happiness and smiled.

"No!", exclaimed Sana incredulously, "I stopped in my tracks; looked up, and hanging from the trees! Swinging sideways...front-ways... above me, were Betsura, Jenday, and Yong-Sun-Sook! Quacking and clucking like ducks or chickens! Quaking and hanging from the trees! Animals!"

"Brraack-brrack-ock-ock"—Yong-Sun-Sook folded his fists into his armpits then flapped his elbows making chicken sounds.

"Very funny," mused Aapep as he hit a mushroom with his thumb and forefinger so that it flew across the table to hit Yong-Sun-Sook in a ringing redness of sting upon the top of his ear.

Sekhet flushed a roll of wine and ale from one goblet to another, shaking the mixture into a frothy mess. She poured the mixture from high in the air into her open mouth to end her eccentrics by making an open-mouthed wet noise like : "gargle-blargle-largle."

Betsura intervened the many smiles with his own latest thrill. It was about one of the endless choices of games they could play. "I played Sushi-Salmon the other day, and I got caught in a spinning mine-cart that never got out of the mush-blossoms, which kept springing up, so I had to start the whole game over!"

"Oh Betsura!"—came many such comments from the table. "So that is why we were all hungry for salmon yesterday! You could have told us!" Thus amid the spattering of happily grumbled comments everyone around grabbed tomatoes, mushrooms, small onions and potatoes, hence pelting Betsura with the bits of food while he tried to shield himself from the edibles flying through the air at him. One small potato stuck upon Betsura's forehead for ever so slight a moment before sliding down slowly. With Betsura picking up the fallen potato for an act of retribution, there alit among the entire group a quick yet very nasty vegetable fight.

"Hey Grolin!" Sana was shouting whilst she stood up. "Is Barlee's arm ready to be eaten yet?"

"Yes!" Grolin examined the arm before looking back up. "Yes, it's ready! But it belongs to Ramley!" Poking the long silver sharp-tongs deep into the arm just above the browning crisping hand, Grolin admired the juices oozing out. He pulled the arm off the tongs with his big bare fingers. "Head's up Ramley! Catch!"

Ramley caught the arm perfectly precise. Everyone whooped 'Yay'! *Ramley and Barlee locked eyes.* Ramley took a huge *tearing* bite out of the arm; chewed three times, then with a grimace of displeasure he spit the flesh out of his mouth over the back of his shoulder.

"Ohhhhh, Barlee!"—Ramley said, "You taste *awful*!"

(He threw away the entire arm over his shoulder whereby it sparkled then disappeared after smacking upon the ground.) Everyone present groaned or laughed, hit the table, spewed or chuckled.

Grolin finally came to the table with a large leg of 'something' to eat. Everyone munched joyfully on their tasties in a sort of slurpy, smacking, silence for a while. Then Miraculum realized they had forgotten to pray before the meal. All present remembered this at once because of their profound connection, putting down their food to bow their heads and clasp their hands as Miraculum began to speak, "Bless this mighty feast. We give thee thanks. And we say a prayer of deep desire for our fallen brethren. Bring them back to be here with us in heaven, that we may at last be at peace and One all together. Amen." Some around the table also said 'Amen' while others snorted more than spoke. Everyone began cheerfully eating again when all at once their smiles faded. In their particular world since they all share one psychic mind amongst one another, if one person feels something then they *all* feel it together at the same time. Suddenly they all felt a deep sadness and longing for their lost brethren. They all pushed their food aside to sit sad and sullen. The sullenness lasted. Miraculum felt the need to pray again. Miraculum began, and everyone bowed their heads. "Some of our brethren went to that place called earth to try and understand the Ones that call themselves the 'Good' and to beat some sense into them..."

Tobias picked up the prayer instantaneously, "...and then others of our brethren went to find our fallen and bring them back..."

Then Barlee spoke instantly, "...so bring them back, please, for we miss them, miss them, and we love, love, love them and need them all back Home to stay."

"Amen"—rumbled everybody at the same time. Yet all at the table continued to sit sad and sullen. They had no idea that on the Good side of the spectrum no-one ever felt sad or sullen, for such things simply did not exist there. They had no idea from very Good Soul's Home-Planets, (and all the spectrums fanning out from there to a *million* different light-rays, from very bright to *many grays*,) even all the way to evil at the deepest darkest other end of a different spectrum of Soul's Home-Planets. So terribly sullen and missing their fallen brethren they simply sat.

Then all of a sudden the entire group lit up with cheer and great excitement, so much so that some even stood up on their feet! Miraculum whom was standing, smiling, beat his chest with his huge muscular fists shouting gleefully, "I have an idea!" All present felt the marvelous buzz of excitement!

"I will go!"—announced Miraculum. "I will check the Akashic Record and find one of our brethren! Then I will go and get them! Then I will bring them back here, and we will all go over the very steps I took to bring them back Home… once we know the steps to bring them back Home, then we can set up an entire party of us and we shall go to this earth place together and bring all our brethren Home at once!"

This was a fabulous, brilliant, idea, thus everyone felt the thrill of excitement! Happiness enveloped them all. There was much rejoicing.

Miraculum strode long strides over to a semi-clear, large, rectangle, that was approximately eight feet tall from the ground, and only six feet away from the bar-b-q grill. He touched the center of the semi-clear rectangle, a bright blue screen glowed. At the bottom of the blue screen were letters, and Miraculum typed in "Akashic Record." Immediately the screen changed color to a delightful purple with the image of a gorgeous old book on it, with a lovely rusty-gold metallic emblem on the front of the book that looked like a metal square with three shining metallic circles inside the square, a silver metal dove in flight on top of the three conjoining rings. An ancient, pristine, observed portrait cheerful to the surveillant oculus.

Hinting a tactile sensitivity that alighted an approbatory fealty fidelity of certitude oblivion he fawned over the exultant sycophantical decorated scroll upon the screen. Miraculum delicately touched the image of the book and it opened to a pleasant cream colored set of pages with ornate letters at the bottom.

Miraculum typed in *"find our good brethren."*

The book glowed with light and grew large until it became pixilated for a moment. Then an image appeared. The image was of a living room in a shoddy house. Dirty white walls with a white ceiling holding one large glowing bulb of light hanging from above without benefit of a glass cover. Strange dirty-brown trod upon carpet that might have once been a dark cream color. A worn muddy-white couch with annoying flower patterns set against the back wall on the right-hand side of the room. Nothing else sat in the room except an old television that played in black and white and had a huge knob on it for turning channels. Even the large boxy square television sat on nothing, it was simply set upon the nasty carpet floor, plugged into an outlet next to it at the wall. The front door was to the left of the television, a kitchen opened up past the wall to the right of the television. A large, white, bald man with no shirt on and a glubby fat belly was on his knees with his trousers and underwear down past his thighs. He had his left hand firmly pressed into the hair of a small, white, girl of age three or four; smashing her face with the weight of his hand into the dirty carpet. [From the image wafted an obvious scent of dog-pee from the carpet; which Miraculum snorted distastefully at as it wafted from the screen.] Miraculum concentrated hard for it was with love he scrutinized the panorama agog with his sacrifice to vindicate a victory that was a conquest and a triumph far greater than a feather in the hat; lives, nay, souls depended on his forthright vigilance. His estimation of the screens display was impractical considering his frame of reference yet he kept a weathered eye open lest he remiss a beloved brethren. Therefore Miraculum keenly stocked his wits to be *prepared against any shocking*

anomalous courtly pretext that could
thwart his general principle of sage
rescue.

On the screen the huge blubbery-
bellied bald man had his right hand upon
the child. She was sky-clad except for a
small pair of white cotton panties tangled
about her bony thighs. The bald blub
man was keeping the four year old girls
body up with his right hand. Suddenly,
as Miraculum watched the screen, the
child went into an epileptic seizure. Her
body shook and her teeth grit. "Get
something!"—the man on her yelled.
The other man who was standing near the
opening to the kitchen shouted back,
"What?"

"Get something to put in her
mouth!"—yelled the offender, "She
might bite her tongue off!"

"She's having a seizure!—yelled the
other man.

"Yes, yes, I know, you idiot! Get something to put in her mouth!"

"What?!"

"Anything! Just get something and put it in her mouth!"

So the other man looked around in a panic, stumbling backward into the kitchen. He looked over, seeing an object, he grabbed a wooden spatula. Shuffling forward in gangly steps he stuck the wooden stirring spoon into the girls mouth whereby she continued to grit and tremor while she bit the wood hard. Coincidentally just as the bald man came to his climax the four year olds seizure stopped. He patted her bottom, pulled up his underwear and trousers, stood up with sweat on his face, neck, and shoulders. His cheeks were flush as he smiled. Leaning down he grabbed the girls panties and zigzagged them back up to cover her. The other man ran off through the living room, past the couch, into the hallway and into a bedroom where he slammed the door shut. The bald man patted his blubbery belly, sighed, stretched his shoulder muscles, then popped the bones in his neck from side to side as he smiled and waddled his way past the couch through the dark hallway to the bedroom at the very end of the hall, which he entered, closing the door behind himself softly.

Miraculum watched the scene on the screen with confusion. An assorted burning discombobulation disproved harmonious gracious coagulation of the events that he was viewing on the screen. He had no concept of sexual abuse; nor utterance of such contemptuous assault; so it meant nothing to him one way or another. Yet he did know there was a bright glow of sweet luminous light around the four year old girls body as her eyes stared fixed and unblinking. Then he watched in perplexed amazement as three soul-parts popped out of the girls body and made their way happily skipping towards the kitchen. Each small part of the child's soul looked just like her except they wore pretty dresses and their forms were see-through like ghosts. The three soul-parts were chatting about wanting to cook something in the kitchen. "I know, let's bake a cake!"—said one.

"Yes!" –exclaimed another—"A birthday cake! What's better than a birthday cake?!"

"Make it chocolate!"—said the third; an obvious favorite flavor that they all seemed to agree upon.

"Yes!"—said the first ghostly soul-part grabbing a boiling pot, "A chocolate cake! Yay!" The three soul-parts seemed quite happy about this, busying themselves about the ratty kitchen. Yet one soul-part that Miraculum had not noticed before, seemed more solid, and was a fourth one that stood staring down at the girls body. The expression on the face of this fourth more solid soul-part appeared both blank and stern at the same time. She looked like the child but perhaps a few years older; wore a cream dress with beige lace on it.

All at once the four year old girls eyes blinked and came to life. She eased herself up into a standing position. She looked sharply to her left where her thin blue-green sheer nightgown lay upon the dirty carpet. As she snatched up her nightgown pulling it over her head the three soul-parts in the kitchen sucked back into her body like the pull of a vacuum cleaner. The nightgown fell over the girls shoulders while the stern, older, and less ghostly fourth soul-part walked *backward* into the child's body, in the same manner of pull, just more slowly.

Having flung the nightgown back onto herself the four year old child ran into the bathroom, flipping on the grimy-coated light and locking the stained fake-gold door. The girl paced about, then went to the sink to tip-toe as far as she could reach, splashing cold water onto her face. Cold, clear, renewing water; God's elixir. She let the wet droplets stay on her skin to sooth her. Then she went to the toilet which looked as if it had not been cleaned in years, and closed the oval lid. Placing her elbows on the toilet lid, she bent on her tiny white knees, clasped her small bony pale hands together, and *prayed* vehemently.

Miraculum watched the scene on the screen both enraptured and agonized at the wondrous sight of the beautiful white light that emanated from the child's soul straight out of her body in a shining glow surrounding her. The *edge-tips* of the light around her body made a perfect circular rainbow of red, orange, yellow, green, blue sky deepening, and purple iris sheen.

Miraculum listened to every word of her insistent prayer most intently. He knew, he just *knew*, that she was one of his brethren. Why else would she have such rapturous beauty of gleaming love light? In his heart he ached with the knowledge that this place of learning made souls 'even-leveled' by putting them in human bodies. Miraculum sighed while thinking that it was a travesty really, because being in human bodies made it hard to tell who was who. Yet Miraculum recognized the brilliant light glowing from the child's soul and out around her body. The powerful unconditional love that vibrated from her soul's-light. Oh yes, she was definitely one of his lost and fallen brethren! He would bring her Home!

Miraculum touched the screen, it faded into blue emptiness, shrunk into a circle to a tiny pin-point, then the image disappeared. Leaving the screen a clear see-through appearance once again, one could see the waving lime-green willows just beyond in the vivid melting greens of the meadow. Miraculum turned to his friends; his family, and with a tremulously grand excitement announced: "I've found one!" Everyone cheered! "I've found one of our brethren, and I shall go to this learning place, bring them back, here, and then we can all go over how I did it!" More cheers blossomed and showered into the air. "Once we know exactly how to bring our brethren back Home, we can form a search-party and all go together to bring every one of them back Home!" -- And there was much rejoicing.

*   *   *

Miraculum strode boldly, with the cheers of his friends bolting through the air. He raised his arms victoriously, everyone around rumbled fabulous encouragement. He turned then to the long clear see-through tube. This tube stood thirty-three feet high and was only a few feet away from the screen he had just been looking at. Bravely, showing insatiable courage, Miraculum tucked his wings close to his body and stepped into the tube. He pushed a button. With a noise that sounded like "thwok" he was pulled with a powerful vacuum force. He disappeared.

* * *

Miraculum was surrounded by smooth to the touch creamy textured slightly warm white light and he felt himself floating, falling, and drifting gently through the light towards a large dark square door that had no handle. The door opened, he was blinded for a moment by a starkly shocking white light. The door closed behind him and disappeared. He landed on his feet in the middle of the very living room he had seen on the screen! He was *here*!—the reality of it bouldering him—he was actually in the place he had seen just previously! Amazement thrilled his senses as he looked about to see that he was in an actual room, in an actual house, in real-time on the planet called earth!

Immediately Miraculum searched out the child. He marched to the bathroom to search for her as she was nowhere to be seen in the filthy dusty living room. Walking through the bathroom door as if it were a glossy fog, he found the child still on her knees next to the toilet with her hands clasped like tiny bony faded white petals, squeezing tensely still in prayer. Miraculum watched as she stood, the four year old, whom ambled over towards the bathroom door. The light with the rainbow tips that shone around the child was fantastically, magnificently, brilliant! He could feel the light from around himself shining, as he leaned his great face towards her, placing his fingertips under her chin, lifting her face towards him.

She saw him! He was deeply humbled by the profundity of it. She truly, actually, *saw* him! Miraculum trembled with the realization that the child felt his hand, his gentle fingertips, underneath her chin; that she saw his hand and saw his face amidst the fogs of waving light. Even though she was seeing just his face and hand only, since his entrance onto earth still left a shining glow of light all around him, there was a most definite and physically tangible buzz like electricity in the air. With his fingers lifting her chin, her brown eyes looking directly into his own eyes he said to the child:

"Well, you're a young one."

The child had heard Miraculum's words. Her languid blinking and

sweetening smile soaked in his warmth.
His words were like manna. The light
around Miraculum faded, seeped away,
like the foam on a beach being tugged
into the ocean. The four year old child in
her shear green-blue nightgown was now
looking past her little pinkish barefoot
toes down at the floor.

Miraculum was in his full body now.
He flexed the muscles of his arms,
exercised his enlarged flank irradiated
precious-opal iridescent dark wings in
wind-gushing flaps, though the child
could no longer see him. He scratched
an itch on one of his horns. Then with
clenched fists, arms upwards and out to
his sides, he *roared with rage* as he
walked through the bathroom door in a
smooth glassy slide, into the dark
hallway of the house; leaving the girl to
stay in the closed bathroom. He
stomped, feather-flapping, and screamed
with rage! The fire of anger lent him to
clench-fisted arms outward as he

pounded his feet in long pestered bangs upon the floor. He passed through the door at the end of the hallway. Inside the bedroom he saw the assaulting bald man laying on a bed underneath a blanket with some woman with spiky plastic rollers in her hair whom was sleeping beside the fat bald man that stunk of acrid rotting sweat and putrid carcass breath. Miraculum lifted his eyes, fists, arms; his eyes glazed with anger and hatred as he screamed, roared again, a thunderously violent sound like a million flapping wings echoing deep and low from some lost wet cave.

Lowering his arms, now fixing his gaze upon the bald man, he stealthily side-stepped in long predatory strides to the side of the bed where the man lay sleeping. Miraculum slowly lowered himself onto one knee and leaned so that his mouth was close to the bald mans ear. In a *whisper* that swelled with the emotions of thundering screaming anger he steamed his words into the mans ear, "You will pay for this! You scum! You *Pig*!" Then Miraculum leaned in closer so that his warm lips touched the mans waxy earlobe. Miraculum gently whispered, "Tonight, you shall die."

Miraculum lifted upward, breathing in deeply through his nostrils. Then he thrust his head and horns into the filmy flesh of the bald mans head, and Miraculum poured out with pestilent force every feeling of fear. terror, and horror, horror, horror, that he could muster, into the mans head! The man *felt* it!

The bald man sat bolt upright, fully awake with eyes huge with fear, stinking sweat dripping from his head, nose and throat; he yelled in terror! The woman laying next to him waved a limp hand at the man and mumbled, "Go back to sleep darling, your just having a bad dream." Her face never left her pillow.

Miraculum thrust his head into the mans head again whereby he flowed forth mighty waves of horror and terror as he repeated over and over into the mans head… "Die! Die! Die! You Pig!"

The man bound up out of the bed with terror rolling throughout his body and soul. He tried to fight it pounding his palms against his head. Miraculum had succeeded and he gloatingly pulled his own head out of the mans head. The mans heart was clenching up, so the blubbery-bellied man pounded his chest, his arms, then began walking in circles pounding his skull. A horror and fear he had never known before enveloped his body, mind, and soul, completely. Miraculum grinned with pride saying, "Now you are mine. You *know* what you must do, if you want to end this writhing horror that is melting your brain!"

Without full realization of how he had
walked there, the bald man found himself
standing in front of his dresser drawer
and slowly opening it. All he knew was
that he had to end this horror; this horror
that he couldn't even name. Sweating
profusely, his face puffed red, his eyes
still wide with terror; not even knowing
that he was feeling the terror of the child,
his scabbed, wrinkled, red-knuckled
hands slowly entered the dresser drawer
beneath his wife's nightgowns. He
pulled out in both his ugly brawny hands
the gun he kept there.

Miraculum grinned with the
satisfaction of a hunt, following the bald
man as he waddled with the gun, loaded,
laying upon his upturned hands. He
followed the man into the garage where
an old tattered lounge chair sat molding
next to a tool bench. The bald man slow-
acting, shaking, lowered himself into the
lounge chair and for some reason
grabbed the handle attached to the side of

the chair, pulling up the handle he lifted the attached foot rest so that his feet were propped up. "Do it!"—whispered Miraculum as if praying siddur. "Do it!"—growled Miraculum. His powdery-cotton winnock of wingtips sinewy brushing the 'pigs' face, he placed his lips against the bald mans ear so that their skin touched, and he hoarsely whispered, "*Die!*"

The bald mans hand held the gun, finger on the trigger, and with great shaking, he brought the gun up to his temple placing the barrel directly upon his skin, then he pulled the trigger! One bullet and a splatter of brain and blood and it was done. Yet miraculously, no-one in the house woke up or even heard the shot!

       *   *   *

----- Miraculum felt his spirit's sails blown weak and limp from reiterating his story that before had only been between himself and God with panting perspiring heartfelt burning to Dr. Roberts whom sat listening and quiet. Yet his momentum was drummed up like Native Americans spelling around a fire, so he did not wish to discontinue thereby ending the hub of his sanctioned confessions. Turning his face towards Dr. Roberts in ruddy genteel declaration he exhumed forbearance despite his reeling gulping uncertainty towards his woebegone wiz of pronounceable phrases. He felt each verbal step was exposing evulse extractions of exanimate fatigue from his heart. Taking in great insensate guzzles of air Miraculum felt glad to finally exult his both blithe and blue true story to the dear Dr. Roberts. With such solace to at last confess his experiences he felt surrounded by a demur glow to share with Dr. Roberts everything. Miraculum realized he wanted to contour his narrative; he wanted to tell more; he wanted to proceed. Thus with sweet courage he continued to tell his story.

THREE

Miraculum felt a pull into a bright white light that dragged him backwards into itself right after the piggish man had killed himself. He felt a floating falling waft, saw a dark door with no doorknob. The door opened. It felt as if he had been set down gently. Door disappearing, his eyes adjusted as the bright white light faded. He found himself in a child's room. It was spotless clean without a single thing out of place, and was terribly empty of any toys, or in fact anything at all that a child might have. It had two pieces of furniture , a bed and a desk. There was a closet painted white with the doors closed. Looking around the room he saw that all the walls were covered in a white wallpaper with millions of clusters of tiny purple flowers flat and lifeless upon it.

"Gag!"—stated Miraculum—"The wallpaper is horrible!"

"Yes. I hate it too." It was the girls soft small voice.

Miraculum turned towards the voice and realized he recognized the child who was in fact sitting at the desk. It was the same child! Only older! It was his beloved brethren! "I wonder what age she is now?", he mumbled to himself.

"I am eight years old," said the child, "And the awful wallpaper is *my* fault. My parents said that as a gift, I could be the one to choose the wallpaper for my room." The girl child of eight sighed. "I wanted wallpaper with purple flowers on it, which is what I told them." She sighed again and pulled a blonde strand of her hair from her eyes. "Since I didn't actually pick it out myself, I had no idea it would be such a constant, repeated, pattern. As a matter of fact, it's so *many* flowers all huddled together that it *scares* me. So I try not to look at it."

"You can hear me?!"—thrilled Miraculum.

"Of course I can hear you;" said the child. She was bland and unsurprised in her demeanor.

Miraculum was so happy he could hardly stand it. Joy filled his heart! He lifted his arm, pulling them back and forth while moving his huge black booted feet forward and forward then backwards and back again in a 'happy-dance'. The sisal of lateral papilionaceous wind-spirit wings shivering silver and blue, and purple, in it's deep blackness stretched back as far as they would go as the feathered tips quivered. Bobbing his chin to a gleeful tune he alone heard in his head. Blessed blissful gaiety had a taste like jelly-beans and a smell like sunflowers, with a lyrical ditty spieling resonantly melodious in his dizzy goosey coconut bosom. Dippy silvery grinning was impossible for Miraculum to evade, so he let the smirk remain while copping an attitude of calm confident virility. Then he moved over past the desk to lean against the wall with trickling tingling joy flooding through him. "So," he said coolly and with macho, "Can you see me?" He was softened ripe with positive expectation.

The girl looked past him; through him. Then she looked all about the room, especially the ceiling. She stood up from her chair at the small desk where she had been coloring unicorns and rainbows with crayons. Going over to her bed with the beige cotton knit blanket tucked and spread perfectly across it she looked underneath it with her small hand lifting the fringes of the blanket to peer beneath. She seemed to look under her bed for a long time against hopeless hope. She stood up. At last she turned in a slow circle looking all about the room; again concentrating especially upon the ceiling. Lingering her eyes upon the ceiling from one corner to the next. Then the eight year old girl with blonde hair straight as paper and big brown eyes with ghostly white skin, walked in a meandering way back to her desk, sitting back down. She picked up a pencil. Sadly and with disappointment, "No," she said, "I can not see you."

Miraculum was heartbroken. She could *not* see him. "But you can hear me still?"—he asked.

"Oh yes. Yes. I still hear you. You sound so sweet."

Miraculums heart bulged with love when she said he sounded sweet. So he positioned himself with his shoulder leaning against the wall, his arms crossed. He smiled while feeling such deep love for her. If only she could see him then she could feel safe and reassured to know he was right by her side; looking at her; loving her with a parents unconditional love…the love of kindness. Soon to take her 'Home'. "So", he said as he peered down to see what she was doing. A book with hard bright pink backing on each side that was filled primarily with empty pages, had pictures beautifully colored with crayons. Amidst the bright and colorful pictures of moons and suns and creatures precious and divine were writings in pencil. "So what are you writing?," he asked.

"A poem."

"Ohhh…," he said and bent low only to become frustrated at the realization that he could not make out her teensy-tiny writing. "So then," Miraculum began, "As you sit there in that human body, you must have a name. What is your name?"

"Amii," said the child as she breathed in with happiness and peace the delicate light of love beaming from the being. She was not afraid even in the least. "My name is Amii."

It was then that Miraculum had a magnificent, brilliant idea! "Stand up!"—he commanded gently, "And face the window opposite your bed."

Amii set down the pencil, flattened her lips for a moment, then she finally smiled while hunching her shoulders with interest. Amii stood up and faced the window; "Okay."

As one of his own sweet brethren all he had to do was jump into her body, make her feel his and his families fantastic unconditional love, remind her of Home, and then 'Waa-La!'—she would come Home with him. Thus Miraculum pounced at her head-first into her body. He was spectacularly surprised! Immediately he was thrown backwards terribly hard, unable to enter her physique at all! He landed on his bum.

"Ow," said Amii as she rubbed her forehead.

Miraculum was taken aback. 'Well, that shouldn't have happened', he said to himself quietly. He was flabbergasted. How could he have bounced right off of her? How could he have not simply slid like a skater on fresh ice smoothly into Amii's body? He should have easily lofted up then wafted down and washed into her veins as lovely as an autumn breeze. The shock throw-back like bounce had a boomerang effect impressively surprising.

Then he had it! He would get a good running start; focus his energy like a massive hemorrhage bloating and pushing, *then* he would enter her body! 'Obviously,' thought Miraculum, 'I must not have been focused.' So he pulled himself, knees first then bum, off of the floor; backed up against the wall where the window hung gleaming in sun and shadows from tall oak trees and green watered lawns beyond it. He breathed and snorted through his nostrils with great intention, determination on his face. Then he took in a very deep breath through his widened nostrils and held the air in his lungs as he focused all his energy. In a massive blow he snorted all the air out of his flaring nostrils, banding a tremendous run at her. He ran with arms straight, hands straight and flat; he leapt at her head!

"Ow!"—hooted Amii again rubbing harder this time at her forehead.

Miraculum was instantly thrust backwards with unimaginable force; this time landing on his bum, sliding several screeching inches then with a swing of gravity fell all the way down onto his back! Raising woozy to a sitting position he felt a whistling loss of his magical

talents, an utter confusion swayed
through him. Salty wetness surged up in
his eyes; dripped in hot droplets down his
thick-skin cheeks. Wiping the tears from
his face with his tender log fingers.
Rubbing his sea-water eyes hard.
Blandishing the back of his hand
repeatedly back and forth under his nose.
"Come Home!"—periled Miraculum in
suffering sorrow—"Come Home!"—he
begged Amii. "Come Home brethren",
he cried, "if only you knew how much
we love you…how much we *miss* you!"

"Ah!"—exclaimed Amii. Her left
nostril lifted in her perplexity as she
massaged her scalp with her fingertips.
"I must be getting a headache," she said
out loud to herself. Then the pain sifted
away. "Oh, bother," stated Amii flatly as
she quoted Winnie The Pooh. Turning
back to her desk she sat down, picked up
her pencil and began writing once more.

"Now that should not happen at
all!"—exclaimed Miraculum regaining

his strength as he bounced back onto his feet. "What's going on?!"—he shouted with sincere questioning at the girl. She had no reaction! She wasn't hearing him. "What's happening?!"— Miraculum practically screamed at the child. Still she gave no reaction. "Hello!? Can you hear me?"—he asked. (Nothing.) "Can you see me?"—he asked. (Still nothing.) Not only could his brethren child Amii not see him, but she could no longer hear him as well? This was unthinkable! Tears bubbled uncontrollably once more in Miraculums eyes. He fell to his knees in the middle of the room. Falling back into sitting he allowed a vanquished sigh to blow from his mouth as he relinquished the back of his hands to fall down onto the floor with a thump. Agony and sorrow yanked at his heart and soul. It was not like any feelings he had ever known before. *Miraculum was having his first real taste of actual pain.* The feelings seemed so foreign and unfamiliar yet he was strong of spirit and would not let them deter him from his purpose! He and his kind had such deep love, such kind, unconditional love for their brethren. It was unbearable not to have them all Home when they recalled their fallen brethrens absence. Miraculum's shoulders shuddered; he began to cry so hard. His crying turned to painful surging sobs. What was this terrible feeling? Not like any sorrow he had ever felt before! Tears flowed down his face as his heart and soul searched for answers. Trying mightily to understand the feelings he was experiencing. "How can I bring you Home?"—he muttered through his sad sobs—"If I can't reach you?" Miraculum cried harder. Then he lifted his hands to the heavens with his palms upward, his arms outstretched as the tears slowed from his eyes. He belted out in desperation, "We love you, Amii!"

The girls head jolted up and she looked at the ceiling. Then she turned with keen listening pretty poised attention, gazing at the ceiling Amii said, "I love you too!"

Miraculum stood to wiped the droll stilling tears from his face. "Can you hear me?" (Nothing; no reaction at all.) Amii had heard him for that sweet precious moment, but no more. "Can you see me?" Once again, nothing. The girl twirled around while looking at the ceiling with joyous tears in her eyes. As far as Amii knew the room was empty now; but she was flowing with sunny happiness at having heard for one brief blessed instant the words, 'We love you.' Amii wiped away her own peaceful tears that had trickled from her big brown eyes, past her ghostly pale skin onto her pink cheeks. She sighed, looking down at the floor as if meditating a warm spring day with the surprise of seeing a wild deer come out from behind a tree in the forest. Like a contemplation of native loveliness and beauty unexpected. Then little eight year old Amii walked

back to her desk but with a skip of
pleasure inside of her, sat down, picked
up her pencil, and began writing again in
the little pink book with empty pages for
her alone to fill.

*　　　　　　*　　　　　　*

Miraculum was standing there looking
at the child at her desk with the pencil
oddly placed between her busy fingers
while he felt confounded. A new feeling
that was an inclination towards nausea
burbled when he was startled to be
sucked backwards into the bright white
light again quite suddenly. He landed
smack dab in the pine-smelling clean
kitchen of the house that Amii lived in;
the eight year old Amii was wearing a
yellow dress with ruffles at the short
sleeves and neck in this new day. She
was sitting at the kitchen table practicing
her mathematic times tables with pencil
in hand and large wide-striped thick
paper upon the vinyl tablecloth that was
spotted with images of strawberries.

Amii's older brother was at the kitchen sink pouring himself a glass of water from the tap.

Miraculum looked at the brother, then at Amii, and had a magnificent, brilliant idea! She needed to come Home with him, he was sure of that, but how to get that task done proved more daunting than he had expected. So! He could kill her! My, my, but perhaps, just perhaps, he could pound her out of that human body of hers! Then he could take her soul by the hand and peacefully, lovingly, *joyfully*, take her back Home! He could kill her!

At once Miraculum shrunk his wings into disappearance to glide back inside the energy of his apparitional backbone; he pounced at the brother and entered his body! The brother had a profound sense of being set back mentally into a dark room, like a dream, whereby it seemed to him as if his body were moving about like that of a puppet on strings.

Miraculum had full control of the human brothers body and he spun fiercely around; his eyes seemingly spitting fire. The fast and violent move of her brother caused Amii to turn around in an instinctual animal sense of fear. Amii looked up at her brother. He was huffing and puffing through his nostrils, his eyes were both glazed and shiny, full of murderous flame at the same time. His shoulders were raised, his arms taut. The hairs on the back of Amii's neck raised up like warning hackles.

Amii stood up and gasped in a breath that did not seem to wish ever again exit her lungs. That glazed, shiny, murderous look in her brothers eyes were all she needed to know that she had better run! Run for her life! Yet her feet stayed plunged to the floor as she awaited her lungs to please, please, exhale! Amii had no idea that this was anyone else but her brother. She had no idea that there even was a Miraculum. Suddenly her lungs exhaled the oxygen, her shoulders jumped; she started to run but her brother caught her with super-human strength. He lifted her by the neck with one hand and slammed her against the wall hard, so that her feet dangled two and a half feet off of the floor! He pulled her back with the mere strength of one hand around her throat and banged her head against the wall. Then he pulled back and did it again. With her feet dangling; granted she was a very thin small girl, he slammed her head against the wall repeatedly. Over and over. Until at last Amii lost consciousness and Miraculum inside her brothers body thought himself triumphant. He let go of her throat. Watched her slide down the wall into an unconscious slump on the floor. Miraculum yanked the brothers body by the shoulder, thrusting it off of him so that the older brother fell onto the floor and looked up at his little sisters heaped unconscious body to become terrified; he wasn't even sure what had happened.

The poor brother, bless his heart, poor
dear, was not at fault at all! He was still
a child himself. Scrambling to his feet as
his mind came fully back to himself, the
older brother knew that whatever it was
that had happened it had terrified him
completely. In fear the boy ran out of the
kitchen and up the stairs to his bedroom
where he slammed the door behind him
and locked the door. Evil was afoot.

Miraculum watched Amii in ecstatic
awe and waited with impatient
anticipation. He waited for the moment
of rapture, of death. Waiting as he
watched he looked for the tell-tale signs
of the rapture; the glowing swirl of colors
as she separated from that puny little
body and looked up at him and *thanked
him*! Then he could finally at long last
take her Home. Miraculum stood with
his feet apart, hands on his hips. His
eyes blinked. His eyebrows lifted. He
waited longer still. Miraculum rubbed
his chin then bent down on one knee next

to the girls body to check and see if she were still breathing. He placed his palm against her chest; then upon her back. He wriggled her toes while looking at her face, then checked for a pulse. It was in endless exasperation that he finally licked his finger then placed it under her nose. It was ever so shallow but she was breathing! Miraculum cupped his hands on her shoulders and for the first time he got an actual taste of real horror… "Alive?!", he screamed. "Alive?!"—he raised his eyes to the heavens shouting. "How can this be?! What is going on?!" Softly then to Miraculums perplexed amazement the girl kept breathing until her chest heaved upwards, and after what seemed a very long time she came back to consciousness! Then Miraculum stood up dumbfounded as of all the bizarre things to do, Amii stood up woozily, tottered to the table, sat back down, to continue practicing her mathematic times tables… (oddly doing far better at it in fact than she had been doing before.)

Miraculum had to pull his mouth shut
from its open lagged position. He was
completely utterly stupefied. Miraculum
did not know that the true reason Amii
went back to doing her times tables was
because she had no clear explanation for
what had happened and honestly could
not think of what else to do. Perhaps,
thought Amii, if she went back to what
she had been doing, then perhaps
everything would go back to being
normal. Miraculum wavered with a
reeling, stumbling backwards; a bright
white light appeared around him without
parade to cuddle and envelope him. He
melted into the warmth and love for only
an instant when without so much as a
word or a message the light released him.
He was supremely crushed with
astonishment. It was at this time that the
bright white light stopped coming for
Miraculum and sucking him into it. Now
he was stuck. He was stuck walking
around after Amii. Following her
everywhere she went. If he even tried to

go to another room he found himself immediately zipped right back by her side. No light; no nothing…just *zip*! To make it worse, he was invisible and mute to her. She could not see nor hear him!

*   *   *

One day, sitting in the kitchen with his elbow on the table and his head resting in his upturned palm, he felt an awful human feeling. He felt *time*. The actual passing of it. The slow innocuous ticking of it. He also felt a most horrible new feeling they do not have in Heaven on his Home-Planet. This particular grating human feeling was sheer and utter boredom. He thought it a most terrible feeling indeed. Miraculum sat there folding then unfolding his foliaceous raven-colored feathered airfoils back and forth while submersed in horrid boring humdrum.

Amii was nine years old now. In the kitchen as he sat terrestrially bored, he looked at Amii with tedious confounded expressions. Amii was over by a box, squatting on the floor at the corner of the backdoor just to the side of him. The box had baby chicks in it. The yellow balls of teetering fluff peeped, chirped, and bent into Amii's touch, loving it when Amii cooed at them; sang to them; petted their soft fluffy heads and backs. Somehow it annoyed Miraculum that Amii thought of the baby chicks as her family. She loved the chicks so much as to actually feel they were not animals nor pets nor holographic images nor anything at all except her actual surrogate family.

To young Amii the baby chicks were as much her friends as her mother, her father, her brothers and sisters as anyone else was... rolled into one. They were her everything; so much more than pets. This annoyed Miraculum to no end but he put up with the nonsense. Amii was a lock-key child whose family were gone a great deal of the time, thus she spent

most of her time alone, which bothered
her not in the least. Yet this day
Miraculum felt particularly humbled by
the slow stuck life he had with the girl
when Amii's mother returned home early
and came into the kitchen, grabbing a
suppers cabbage out of the refrigerator
and set it onto the cabinet, then took out
a cutting board from the cabinet; putting
her fingertips slowly on the top of a
marvelously large gleaming butcher
knife. Miraculum once again had a
magnificent, brilliant idea!

Miraculum's face lit with excitement!
In magnanimous humility he would not
let down his brethren child, and would do
anything necessary to bring her Home to
the true dignity that he knew they both
deserved. Why hadn't he thought of this
before? Perhaps he could *scare* Amii out
of her human body! With a grrrr of pure
devotion and esteem from the corner of
his mouth, he jumped up with massive
intention. He literally took a dive into

the mothers body! Entering her like smooth water. With a wicked grin he turned around towards Amii to puppeteer the mothers body like warming up for exercise by raising the mothers arms half up, then popping the mothers knuckles; then twitching her fingers.

[It is here in this pontification of his life's events that Miraculum paused to look with weak wet eyes at Dr. Roberts. For his confessions were in need of sympathy so greatly that he wished for water, *some fantastic baptismal font to wash his hands of blood and quench the dry-heat of his parched throat*! Yet as if to drink his pride, he addressed the internal glacial retreat in shy raised tongue to the roof of his closed mouth. Prodding away his fear of verbal illumination by shrewd sly swallowing. He decided to keep speaking, keep confessing; bare his soul. Continuing to tell his story with pedantic bold-hearted bravery, he did not ask for water.]

In the mothers body he slunk over and picked up the box of baby chicks. Amii requested, "What are you doing?"—she looked up at her obviously changed mother. Her mothers entire face had changed, her eyes had a glazed, shiny, murderous glaring fire in them. Amii gasped as she stay squatted upon the floor where the box of chicks had been. She didn't know what to say; she didn't know what to do. Amii wanted to run but her body wouldn't let her go anywhere so long as her mother had that look in her eyes, with her face changed; the box of her fluffy babies in her hands. Amii's mother took the box of chicks over by the sink, pushed away the cabbage, set the box upon the counter. Then the grown woman with that murderous look still in her eyes, and that wicked grin still on her face, placed the cutting-board so that it lay next to the sink. Miraculum smoothed the mother's hand across the board, looked Amii in the eyes and smiled a most horrible smile. Then the mother took the large silver butcher knife, sliding it out from the standing wooden block that held it. She grabbed a chick in her left fist, placing it sideways on the chopping board. She lifted the butcher knife so much higher in the air than necessary and looked Amii directly in the eyes. "What are you doing?," asked Amii whom had now followed so that the young girl was standing in the middle of the fake-tile floor just in front of her mother. Mother said nothing but only gleamed that fire from her eyes while wickedly smiling. Then Miraculum in the mothers body chopped off the heads of the chicks one by one, until the blood flowed off of the cutting board and dripped in thick red lines pooling onto the floor. Amii could not speak. In fact, to Amii's astonishment she could not move. Not a muscle. 'Like a deer in the headlights'; Amii swooned the petrified meandering thought. She tried to move her small bare feet but it was as if they were glued to the floor. Then with a wave of nausea Amii fainted.

When Amii awoke she was still laying on the floor of the kitchen in the spot where she'd passed out. Yet the floor had been cleansed. The cutting-board and butcher knife had been meticulously cleaned and sat now in the sink. The kitchen counter too had been wiped clean, the entire room reeked of bleach-cleanser. But the box was gone. Amii had lifted herself up, looked around, yet the box full of her soft peeping babies was gone no matter where she looked. She could not stand to believe that what had happened *really* had happened. So she hoped and prayed uselessly in her head that it wasn't true. Amii had run into the living room looking for her babies. Then she had run quickly into the piano room looking for her babies. At last she ran in a dither back into the kitchen only to bump into her mother (who was still not her mother at all inside but was Miraculum; disappointed his brethren child had not died of shock yet.) Amii pulled back speechlessly with her mouth opened wide looking wild-eyed at her mother. This strange tall woman still had the burning fatal gleaming glaze in her eyes; still smiling insanely wicked. "Wh… Where are my babies?," Amii managed to stutter out. "The ch..chicks..the box of chicks are gone."

Her mother laughed. It was such an evil laugh that it caused the girl to shudder. "Well, I don't know", said Miraculum in the mothers body, "Perhaps the dog got them!" Then mother slapped her leg and laughed! Laughed so wickedly hard that in fact it made Amii begin to walk very, very slowly backwards. Mother inched up on Amii as the nine year old slowly walked backwards, until the mother's face was nose to nose with Amii's face (so that less than an inch were between them.) Amii stood still as a shocked timid mouse watching her mothers face so close to her own. Then Miraculum spoke again through the mothers mouth to say in the woman's voice but with a tone that sounded to Amii like *pure hatred*, "Why don't you go clean your room?" Mother said, "Go clean your room, and be sure to move your bed so you can clean underneath it. *NOW*!"

"Yes, Mam!"—responded Amii out of flawless fear. Amii ran up the stairs and did not dare defy her mother for fear of something worse! Amii pulled the vacuum out of the upstairs closet; retrieved the puffy duster. Miraculum left the mothers body, flying fast to watch Amii in her bedroom; to see if the child's heart would stop at any minute from fright, the rapture of death would come; but he would be coldly disappointed to find himself only left puzzled while shaking his head. The young child dusted everything in her room, then vacuumed the floor. Now for

moving the bed to vacuum the carpet
which had sat unattended underneath.
Amii pulled and tugged with all her
might at the white painted wood bed.
She shoved sweating heaves at the small
posts of the heavy bed to try and move it,
eventually inch by inch it moved a little.
Then in her sweating huffing breaths
Amii decided that perhaps it would be
easier to push again on the bed rather
than pull at the posts. So she got on the
other side of it and pushed very hard. It
moved! So she pushed again. It was
then that Amii caught sight of something
dark red on the beige carpet of the floor
just underneath the bed where she stood.
Her heart leapt with an odd clenching
fear, she could feel her hands shaking.
What was that?!

Amii got down on her hands and knees
then peered beneath the bed. In a blood-
soaked ring were the heads of her baby
chicks in a perfect circle. Stunned, Amii
silently crawled backward from the bed,

then lifted herself to her feet stealthily. She ran over to her screen-less window. She opened the window, climbed out onto the upstairs roof, wrapped her arms around her knees, and stared up at the blue sky, trying to cry. Yet the tears would not fall…they just brimmed up and stung her eyes.

Miraculum stole out onto the rooftop, sitting down beside her with his own arms wrapped around his bent knees. He felt overwhelmed with confusion; painfully saddened.

[Miraculum perceived an elephantine weight within his ears and he could hardly look at Dr. Roberts for the beginning of his story was so elemental and lacking in his now current preference for a lace-sleeved elegance, he immediately thought it a six-foot snow December in his mind, so dearly in fact that the cold shook off whereby his thoughts inclined a wish for it to be Christmas with sparkling tree-topped

glittery chandleries. Chanceful at that
moment when he had this fancy wish
Miraculum looked over to the corner
near Dr. Roberts bookshelf in her office
to see a glass winged Christmas cat with
a gold loop on its back hanging from the
edge of a photograph containing the
wistful pretty image of a calico kitten.
*He had not far to go in his tale and this
spritely sight bolstered the chamber of
his bravery*, thus he let his voice remain
to be heard by the Doctor. No matter any
stupefied audacity, he continued!]

FOUR

Amii became riddled with night terrors. She would even sneak down to drink some of her father's instant coffee with high hopes she could stave off sleep and thus avoid the terrifying dreams; this was to no avail. The terrible dreams came anyway when at last she could stay awake no longer and her body gave in to unconsciousness and frightening slumbers. Of all things ironic the one dream that did not frighten Amii (*the* dream she dreamt every single night for *two weeks in a row*) was the only one that interested Miraculum! Yes, poor Amii was at a loss, left encumbered with discombobulation at this particular dream; for not only did she dream it every single night for two weeks in a row when she was nine years old, but every single *detailed bit* of the dream repeated itself each night perfectly without changing even in the least! The first part of this repeating dream she saw a black and white television where a newscaster was talking about things (that at this time in Amii's life and in all of history in fact) simply did not exist... nor could anyone imagine such things existing. The newscaster talking about such ridiculous things as a hole in the ozone layer; many species going extinct; gadgets small that people could use as telephones that required no attached wire cord and other such fancies that people could play entertainment games upon; and other small gizmos that one could listen to music on without even needing a record and it's needle on a player to go round the record grooves so that the music played; televisions that were flat of all impossible things! And that is not all! The newscaster spoke of terrible disasters; and some sort of panic causing people to flee! Then next in this

recurring dream a woman whom looked
similar to her Grandmother, if her
Grandmother were about twenty years
old, walked up to Amii whom seemed to
be a full adult already and said to her it
was "Time to go." At this point in the
dream she was on an airplane of some
sort that took her to a huge space craft.
Amii walked onto the space craft (that
looked in it's center as if one were living
in a shopping mall) and she had to make
an important decision that others seemed
hard-placed to make; she then sat down
alone and looked out of a large window
from the space craft and saw what was
either the earth completely blowing up to
smithereens or was something like an
asteroid in front of it which exploded
making it appear the earth blew up. In
finality the space craft took off in what
Amii felt was something like a black
hole. Now what bothered Miraculum
was that Amii would shout loudly in her
sleep during this dream, "You know
what?!" Amii's brother had come flying

out of his room once after many days of
this happening, turning on his little
sister's bedroom light and shaking her
body asking, "What?! Tell me what?!
What is it?!" Yet Amii only mumbled
the answer. This is the very thing that
ever night for two weeks in a row had
eaten at Miraculum…what was Amii
yelling about? What did it mean?!
Miraculum had shouted each night back
at the child the same frustrated words as
her brother that one time. Miraculum
heard Amii yelling, "You know what?!"
And Miraculum shook her body and
pranced frantically around, wanting to
know… WHAT?—Tell him what?!!
Always the child mumbled the answer,
which bothered Miraculum to no end.
He never did find out the answer, but
always felt that whatever it was, it was
very important! Miraculum never would
forget this; and it would never stop
unpleasantly disturbing him.

One night Amii had another terror dream that her family had all taken some drug and had turned into blood-thirsty rabid gorillas with sharp-tipped teeth filling their mouths and had come bursting into her bedroom with fire-glazed eyes and ate her alive. She awoke from the dream to turn on every light in the house (excepting her families bedrooms) just to feel some sense of safety. This would be a waste of money, she knew, to have so many lights on, so she simply hoped nobody would wake up until she had the chance to calm down. The haunt of gnawing mediating nocturnal panoply was an oppressing turbulence that flitted at her mind like a fly that would not shoo but kept coming at her to buzz its annoying anarchy and predispose the demagogue of her rabbity inner self.

She had left the bathroom door open quite absentmindedly as she splashed her face with cold water from the tap.

Precipitous descending water cascaded into the surge of her hands to dilute the cataract rust from her wastrel soporificly exhausting lotus-eating dreams.

She was now *eleven* years old. The noise she realized must have inadvertently awakened her father. Amii's ears pricked and felt hot at the tips like the rising vibration of an off-key soprano had stormed a ballad of forewarning feverish heat intensifying from her earlobes upward. *She did not know the horrors* **would soon be over** *once that night had passed. If she could just make it through that night!* Her father came storming out of his bedroom, looking about he said, "Why are all these lights on? Your wasting money." Amii looked up from the bathroom sink. She didn't even feel like drying the water from her face. In fact, the wet drops on her skin actually felt good, cooling. She just looked up at her father sadly silently. "Did you have a bad dream?"—he asked.

Without speaking a word, Amii merely
shook her head 'yes'. Seeming quite
sympathetic her father said, "Well, would
you like to come in here and sleep with
your mother and I?" His sympathy was
reassuring thus Amii shook her head
'yes' again. She watched from where
she stood as he buzzed about turning off
unnecessary money-wasting glowing
bulbs of light. Then he was back again
where Amii stood leaning against the
doorway of the bathroom. Her father
opened his arms in gesture towards his
marital bedroom. With painful
exhaustion aching in her bones and
muscles from lack of sleep, Amii
followed.

He pulled back the covers gesturing
for Amii to get in the bed to lay between
he and her mother. So with slow drained
tiredness Amii climbed into the bed and
lay facing her mother, feeling that
perhaps she might be able to get some
rest. Her father climbed in the bed

behind her pulling up the covers.
Miraculum, whom had been stuck
following Amii around for all these years
was fraught with exasperation and
boredom. As Miraculum stood in the
marital bedroom to look up at the dark
lamp upon the side table next to the bed,
he himself suddenly had a fantastic light-
bulb of an idea go on in his mind! He
realized he might have the solution to get
his beloved brethren Amii to finally
leave her human body at last, and in true
pure love-light come Home with him to
Heaven. Just as the father was reaching
his arm behind his head to rest it on the
pillow Miraculum jumped exactly like a
child doing a cannon-ball swimming pool
splash and slid directly into the father's
body. The jolt caused the father to flick
his arm up so that he knocked the edge of
the bedside lamp causing it to teeter but
then wobble back in place without
falling. For Miraculum had suddenly
recalled that when he first saw his poor
beloved brethren Amii at four years old

on the Akashic Record screen back on his Home-Planet Heaven, she was being harmed (a word he now vaguely understood the meaning of) by that horrid Pig of a man! The whole assault had brought on an epileptic seizure in Amii so that she had at least four small parts of her soul pop out of her body! Perhaps that had been the hidden secret all along! Perhaps, at last, he could get her out of her body, finally with all the love in his heart, take her back Home to Heaven!

[Miraculum paused here in his story to wipe the salty weeping clear liquid from his eyes and contemplate his courage to tell this final candid electrostatic generator of replevin that was the exuviation votive tensing away his judgment to see the beauty of life. Did he have the courage? At once he had the facetious urge to bolt out of the room, wander beneath the baby-blue sky of the sidewalks in the city. Yet he polarized

his poise to conceal his true inner
urgency and attempted a poker face to
dull his sudden tangent.

Miraculum looked at the salmon
colored walls of Dr. Roberts office, then
raised his eyes as if with interest at the
dark blue ceiling. When he glanced over
to the corner of Dr. Roberts boat-shaped
bookshelf he was anew with surreptitious
astonishment to see once again the glass
angel-cat that hung from a book that even
more surprising he realized now had a
picture of a dog on the cover. The dog
was hefty with fur so as unmistakably to
be a Husky, it held its long noble nose
high with family protection like a luxus
loyal sentient as a wolf would have for
its pack, the soft gentle nanny-bred eyes
like a big-hearted Saint Bernard. This
seemed a sign that concisely epitomized
the cumulative sum of courage, he knew
he could speak the final bits of his torrid
tale. His sensitivity of soul could
withstand the last confession here.

Release of his life's truth would bring again the hope with simple cooling equinox of springtime to the universe. Deep breath of fortitude into heaving lungs he drew his courage forward and continued to tell his story.]

So in the fathers body Miraculum grabbed the thing hanging between the human fathers legs which he found to his relief had been made hard when he'd jolted the flesh by jumping into it, he rubbed it up against Amii's bare backside beneath her nightgown trying to find the rectum thing. Amii froze in horror as she felt her father rolling his unmentionable with the direction of his hand around her backside. She froze uttering to herself, 'It's a mistake. He doesn't really mean to be doing this; he's just in some sort of sleep state and it will…stop…*now*!' Most unfortunately it did not stop for the father got the phallus half-way into her intestine recta with a single tearing hurting hard push. Miraculum was

terrified all at once as Amii *did not pop out of her body* but instead bolted forward, away, onto her feet out of the bed and screamed at the top of her lungs—"Owwww! That *hurts!*"
Suddenly fearing for the first time in his life that there really was 'wrong' and that he himself had just done something 'wrong', Miraculum popped out of the fathers body with a new taste of fear, even actual horror. Miraculum stood back shakingly frightened.

The mother swung up out of bed in a flush of fury swinging the covers away in a huge blanket waft and was on her feet in an instant! Amii ran, stumbled, and then crawled as fast as she could to the toilet in the parents master bedroom. Flinging up the toilet lid Amii wretched and vomited until nothing was left in her stomach. Then she wracked with painful muscle spasms in her back, shoulders, and neck, with empty dry-heaves of spittle until her body forced wads of thick green bile to purge out of her mouth into the toilet bowl. She could hear her mother shouting at the angry bewildered father, "I know why your doing this! You're doing this to make me feel like I'm not pretty anymore! You're doing this to make me feel like you don't want me anymore!" Amii was flabbergasted that her mother was screaming out such a thing. Shouldn't her mother be worried about what just happened to her daughter?

Unexpectedly the telephone rang. The father angrily flustered stomped over to the telephone, picked up the receiver and shouted with wrath, "What?!!" There was a pause as he listened to the little old lady on the other end of the line. "I don't care if you're having problems!"—he screamed into the phone while Amii on the carpet just past the toilet bowl, Miraculum shaking, and the mother furious, watched him. It was one of his patients. "I don't care!"—he screamed into the receiver again, "It's three o'clock in the morning! Well fine! Go find another Doctor if you don't like it!" Father then slammed the receiver back down with a harsh bang!

"Look at that!"—shouted the mother. Amii realized the mother was talking to *her*. Talking to her as she fell back in a hurried crawl bending over the toilet again wrenching out more of the foul-tasting bitter green bile from her mouth. Amii looked up at the mother. Amii was panting, sweating, shaking. Amii tried with a trembling back of her hand to wipe away the greenish drool from her mouth as she sat helplessly limp on the floor leaning against the toilet staring at her mother in astonishment. "What do *you* think?"—the mother poised the question to Amii directly. "What do *you* think Amii? Wasn't that rude of your father to just hang up on one of his patients like that!?" Amii couldn't believe her mother was asking such a question after what just happened. Did she actually expect an answer? It was obvious how both parents stared down at her that indeed the mother *did* expect an answer.

Not knowing what else to do, Amii felt obligated to answer. Shaking her head 'yes' then stuttering out loud, "Yes, tha…that was rude." Amii had told the truth then bolted for the door; running like mad. She ran as fast as she could down the hallway into her bedroom, slamming the door shut and locking it in sheer horror. Miraculum followed Amii, as he stood in the young girls room, he too trembled with horror. Miraculum felt as a burglar who had swindled and pilfered to protract a roborant tonic for the stalwart problematic enigma that was a hasty rebellion against his loyal patrimony patronage. Beating like a watchword his heart rock-ribbed in a flourishing mountain of insensible undulation. This was a pickle of bombasting vaunting clamor. His golem essence abounded in bebouldered rolling quakes. Tremors shook a seesaw tempo of wincing trembles in his body. Triumphant luring sirens, to save his brethren in a trumpet victory towards the loving treasure-house was wanton mashed! He never really knew what 'horror' actually was before. Yet this was not a sense of anything 'Fun'…this was something terrible. This was something ghastly. Somehow for the first real time ever in his life Miraculum knew…he *knew* that he had done something very, very *wrong*. Only he didn't know why it was wrong. *Not Yet.*

FIVE

Many years after that last awful incident Miraculum simply stayed stuck by Amii's side. Watching her go through years and years of therapy. His tenacious listening of the turnstile tussock that was psychotherapeutic thaumaturgics was a theater of the absurd until Amii was treated in a manner for what was deemed '*trances people live*'; this, Miraculum found to be a valid therapeusis which actually relieved and healed the girl. Miraculum thenceforth felt a theocentric dansant apropos for theosophy which he ran wounded towards with vorticity. He did notice that as time went by it became harder, fulsomely more difficult to emerge his wings at will; yet at this point he simply considered this anomaly of ailment to just be an insignificant annoyance. Only once had he broke down and messed up since that last horrible tremulous night.

Amii was turning eighteen, would soon be moving out of her families house. She had planned to move temporarily into her grandmothers empty house while she went to higher education at the nearest university. Miraculum was there trying to amuse himself with little antidotes on where he thought this poster or that mirror should be hung as he watched Amii, knowing sadly that she couldn't hear a word he was saying. It was then that Miraculum had a thought by which it occurred to him that Amii once on her own would be having fun. This brought upon Miraculum without prelude a new emotion which they did not have in his Heaven…jealousy. Jealousy!—He knew somehow that's what it was, but he couldn't help himself. Frustration overtook Miraculum so that

he flew into a rage; jumped into the
mothers body (she had been helping
Amii unpack garage-sale china in the
grandmothers house) and Miraculum in
the mothers body began shouting, "I hate
you! Is that what you want to hear?! I
hate you! I hate you!!" Then he took
absolutely anything and everything that
was breakable. He smashed them to
pieces on Amii's body…glass, dishes,
cups, worn china, lamps. Until he'd run
out of things to break on her; so he began
kicking her and kicking her over and
over again. He only stopped when he
realized that Amii was unconscious.
Then he saw something horrid that he
had never seen before. Parts of Amii's
body were swollen up to become
elephantiasis-like huge. Her body did
not just have spots that were bruised a
black purple, but were completely totally
deep dark black. Miraculum picked up
Amii's unconscious body to lay her
down gently upon the living-room couch,
propping pillows around her; he patted

her hand softly while begging her to wake back up and be okay. He wept great tears of sorrowful weeping grief.

When she awoke he could hardly contain his relief. He continued to cry while patting her hand as she watched him. Miraculum found himself saying repeatedly, "I love you. I love you. But it's *you* who make me do these things. *You* make me do this." Through the seeping tears in his eyes he saw the mixture of pain and fear in Amii's eyes. When she said, "I love you too, Mother;" Miraculum realized with a sudden shock that Amii still had no idea of his existence. To Amii, she was simply looking at her mother. Miraculum let out a sob and kissed her forehead then stood up to walk away.

Out of honest sincere pity, Miraculum walked the mothers body out of the house, got in the mothers car, drove to the store where he walked in, picked up a blue hand-held shopping basket, then

exiting her body he left her there. The
mother would never have any memory of
what had actually happened, or indeed of
why she found herself shopping at the
grocery store. As Amii sat sorely on the
couch back at the grandmothers house
her desire to stay in the house of a
grandmother she dearly loved while
going to school at the closest university
died. It died like a dream down the
drain, flushed. She wanted to move
someplace far, far away now. A big city
with bright lights parading unusual
interesting people. Now it was all a
matter of trying to figure out how she
would make her way to a big city. (Once
she had recovered from her injuries.)

        *   *   *

    Miraculum continued to watch
Amii go through the therapy of
'trances people live'. He watched it's
healing factor as she traveled around
the country. As he watched, waited,
listened, he came upon a frightening

epiphany of enlightenment. Amii was kind and loving, definitely, but she was also very different in so many ways from *his* kind. There were things he liked about her, particularly her odd sense of goofy humor, the strength and courage that was different from anything he'd known before. He had stopped his self-pity, his worry that he might never go back Home. For true interest had enveloped as he came to the enlightenment that perhaps 'the others' who called themselves the 'Good' really were 'Good' in a way that was greatly different from his own kind. Perhaps these 'Good' really *did* exist! He could see now why the 'Good' would think of himself and his kind as 'Evil'; even though they did not think of themselves as 'Evil'. Miraculum could see now why the 'Good' would think of his Heaven as 'Hell' even though to him it most certainly was not.

Walking the mothers body to the store leaving her there out of pity's sake was the first time fate had allowed him to venture away so far from Amii's side. He realized now why 'they' called his kind 'Demons'. He also knew at last why he could never enter Amii's body. Amii was in a human body but her soul was not human and did not belong to earth any more than his did. Yet being a very different kind of creation Amii was what the very 'Good' called a true 'Angel'; she had come here to help people in some way. With this enlightenment, this illuminating knowledge, he knew there really was a spectrum of many, many Kingdoms from one side of the spectrum all the way to the other. Miraculum, for the first real time, truly knew _Who_ he was and _where he belonged_.....(_in the spectrum of things._)

With this knowledge Miraculum discovered he was able to walk farther and farther away from Amii. Yet where would he go? He would just have to take his scary unknown chances; do his best. One warm-air balmy night Miraculum bent down, kissed Amii lovingly on her forehead while she lay sleeping with just a sheet and a fan blowing upon her to keep her cool. She gasped, her eyes fluttered as she put her fingers to her forehead then smiled. She had _felt_ his kiss! "I really do love you Amii," said Miraculum in a hushed humble voice, "and I wish you well." Amii smiled in her smooth dreamless sleep. Miraculum walked away from her at last. Freedom. He walked outside without the information for what his future would truly hold for him other than that he would make it out to be as close to what he wanted while trying not to worry about the small things on this earth; entertain himself with books and movies; watching life go by. Hopefully this was the end of the road. There was a bitter-sweet sadness betwixt joy running through him like an audible bustling humming zing. Rose-colored auspicious reverence elevated the heavy concern in his heart; it looked like he would conclusively go Home. He hoped.

The crowning genesis of the moment contained a conservative revelation of resignation. A residue like oily elderly burnt nectar from antiquated flower blooms that should have long since perished. Their odorous pungent petals still in refection to draw in the innocent hummingbird against all odds of time-worn weariness.

Miraculum strolled into the bromidic bane and musk scented

nights vaporous wind. Maintaining
his walk he half expected at any
minute to become spiraled enlaced by
a whorl of energy that would drag him
back to Amii's flank. Step by intrepid
wondrous fretful step Miraculum was
not snatched back. He kept walking!
He came to a park, a children's
playground, with merry-go-round
shining silvern in the luminescence of
the full-polished moon yawning
broadly in the sky. Swing sets
brushed lightly to and fro, their thick
seats squeaking un-oiled by robust
coiled chains. Tall slide with
impossible steps of a toilsome ladder
that stood towering statuesque; the
spotted light glimmered on it's green
painted-over with blue, painted then
upon red blotches of wane color. He
stopped in the green yellow grass that
rose up past the base of his dark
boots, looked up at the sparkling
diamond stars twinkling in loneliness
or in paucity patterns here and there.

Incandescent brilliance of scintillating starry luster's dots sprinkled the nocturnal ebony sky above him.

A massive glowing bright white light appeared to the right of him! 'I'm going Home at long, long last,' he said to himself, thus Miraculum walked straightly firm towards the light.

SIX

The massive blinding gleam of engorged bright white light was like a telamon of considerable height just to the right of Miraculum at the children's playground. With joy beginning to boom in his thudding heart he walked into the white light thinking to himself that he would go Home, tell all his brethren everything. All he had learned would come pouring from his mouth and soul so that each could feel it with him; vehemently he would warn them all to never, ever go to the learning place called earth. He was going Home!

Miraculum stepping into the light felt a powerful suction pull while hearing a noise that sounded like 'thwok'! He was

enveloped, cradled, by the peaceful light.
All at once without warning the light
began to dwindle. He was shocked to see
himself sitting in the seat of a rusty old
beat-up sunbird car. Miraculum looked
about him in dismay and horror. The two
windows of the car were rolled down so
that the hot air whapped at his face and
horns. Torrid baking wind fulminated
throughout the car like a sweltry fever.
Looking out the window of the moving
car he saw…absolutely nothing really.
Barren endless scorched land. Green-
yellow scalded cactus scattered spotting
the arid territory. Drowsy tumbleweeds
flipping in a treeless blistered landscape
of miles and miles of dirt. The sky,
however, was an ever-stretching skillful
display of pretty blue hues, cotton-puffs
of clouds vaunting beautifully pompous
hanging low as lofty monuments.
Confusion vexed and pelted him as
heated indomitable thrashing wind whirl-
blasted the innards of the car in it's
velocity.

Whipping his head away from the window to his left he took in a long drink of the driver at the wheel. He stared in befuddled awe profoundly disappointed at an older Amii, around age twenty-one he guessed, driving the car. She was listening to a recording of the "Mamas and the Papas", tapping her fingers happily on the steering wheel in beat to the tune, gleefully singing along; only instead of singing 'Cass' she was singing 'cats'. "And after every number they'd pass the hat...," she was singing, "...and no-one's getting fat except mamma *cats*..deedle-da-dee-dee-doodle-dee-dee.." Miraculum weakly lifted his arms with the palms of his hands facing flat upward, he looked up to the heavens (which was really just the inner roof of the old beat-up sunbird); he *screamed*: "I'm in hell!" Then he squeaked out very meekly, "Help!"

Miraculum looked across his whereabouts again then smacked his forehead with his palm; trying very, very hard not to have a panic-attack. Breathing heavily he found himself squinting whilst batting his hands at the hot air blowing like a hurricane from the open windows. "Why on earth are the windows rolled down like this?!"—he yelled.

Amii's shoulders jerked, she looked down at the radio; then took a nervous peek into the backseat. Grimacing, she shook her head. This had happened before whereby her angel guides had spoke to her yet she always found it disconcerting since it would come out of nowhere, add little in the way of great knowledge then leave her ears just as quickly as it came. "Because there's no air-conditioning of course! Why do you think? The air-conditioner's broke!"— Amii said out loud.

"You can hear me?"—Miraculum asked loudly against the battling hot wind thrusting around the car.

"Of course I can hear you;" said Amii as she pressed her lips together frowning hard. Such moments were always incidents of uncertainty. "Great," said Amii with whimsical vexation, "now I'm talking to myself… and… hearing… voices." Lifting an eyebrow and one corner of her mouth, she couldn't help feeling this was all a din of hullabaloo. When this had happened to her as a child it had ended quite abruptly so she thought that perhaps this nostrum balderdash would also end as unceremoniously.

Miraculum leaned whisper close to Amii bellowing mordaciously boomingly loud just to make sure she heard him: "Where are we going?!"

"To Phoenix of course! What do you think?"

Miraculum was terribly confused; "What is a Phoenix? Do you mean the bird?"

"No!" Amii wrinkled her brow. "To Phoenix, Arizona. Shouldn't you be the all-knowing one? Shouldn't you know that? I've been working on my higher education, and taking jobs where I can get them. I've got a gig there. Good grief!" Amii rolled her eyes still managing the steering wheel with her right hand, she placed the fingertips of her left hand on the bridge above her nose between her eyebrows trying to rub the wrinkly frown away.

Indeed it was a genuine fact that Amii was slowly getting her higher education whilst making a living on stage as a comedian. Well...*barely* making a living...the concise un-flowery reality that Amii was nevertheless proud of defined an unfortunate technicality that she was actually living far far-far-far below poverty level, yet what she concentrated upon was that she was a *comedian* and being *paid* for it! This was something she felt worthy of plume and crow for anyone who was an entertainer.

Miraculum leaned in unpretentiously with dearest sincerity shouting, "What's a higher education as opposed to a shorter one?"

Amii snorted incredulously, let out a very deep sigh of surrender: "I'm not even going to bother to answer that! That's ridiculous!" Then she added, "For peats sake!" She again found herself peevishly attempting to rub the frown away from the bridge of her nose. She didn't want the little spot to wrinkle up; after all what if the wrinkle refused to smooth back out just staying there one day!

Miraculum suddenly thought of a most important question he had been wanting to ask regarding life and the nature of the universe. Seeping ever tighter to Amii's ear he brayed a monumental sepulcher of the most weighty important visionary questions to her! (No response from the girl.) Amii in a terrible moment of morbid irony didn't appear to hear anything. The discomfiture was irking so Miraculum tried again; the hot wind whapped his words into an empty moratorium. Thus with irritation Miraculum shouted: "Hello! *Hello?* HELLO!" Nope. Nothing. Exasperated Miraculum gave up with a moody slap on his thighs, snarling a disgusted snort. A remake of Connie Francis's song "Who's Sorry Now" was now blasting from Amii's recording; the tune playing..."Who's sorry now....Who's sorry now..Who's sad and blue...Who's crying too...Just like I cried over you...Boo Hoo..." Folding his hands behind his head he tried to get comfortable. (He couldn't get comfortable.) So he tossed this way and that, wishing he could pull the seat back some. Finally fiddling around the edges of the car seat he found a knob then pulled it extremely hard.

Amii instinctively jumped and shrieked as the empty passenger seat next to her suddenly flew all the way backward down so monstrously hard that the head-rest hit her luggage in the back seat. She eyed the vacant passenger seat, tried to rub her frown away.

Miraculum covered his eyes with the tips of his silky wing gliders in attempt to sleep. It was more of a 'I'm here, but I'm trying not to be' sort of meditative blankness. He thought that perhaps, just perhaps, he might be becoming depressed. The car drive was actually quite long, but for some reason, because of the meditative blankness no doubt, the trip seemed to go by marvelously quick for Miraculum. For Amii, who secretly detested long drives anyway, this was not so. To her it most definitely felt like an achingly intolerably outstretched long-long-long drive. When she finally came to a halt in her journey Amii absentmindedly pulled the emergency brake before stopping; the entire body of the car jolted. Miraculum found himself waking up in fast mid-slide straight down into the passenger floorboard! His knees were crunched up against his head. "Aaaaah", he screamed. Then he moaned a most perturbed moan and rubbed his face. It was like a snail trying to wrench itself out of it's shell for Miraculum to extract himself out of the floorboard back into the car seat. Miraculum's wings had flapped out in a vapid rapid whomp when he fell, individual spirituous feathers fluffed off abandoning his wings like long membranous spinsters lost. He watched them fall in seesaw waves and blew on one so that it skirted up only to fall back down on his nose. Such a thing had never happened before, yet he did not worry as to if it were normal or not.

Miraculum lifted his gaze to peer out of the window as the car came to a more settling halt. He saw one of the most beautiful sunsets he had ever laid eyes upon. It was an awe of salmon, pink, soft and dark blues, orange flaming, wildly soothing melting magenta. Amii got out of the car as Miraculum simply walked *through* the car. They stood side by side in front of the old beat-up car's hood gazing out at the peeking flowing beauty of color falling down to the horizon in the behemothic sky. ---- "Awwww," sighed Amii. "Awwww," sighed Miraculum. Behold the lovely languid bel-canto of the sunset heavens!

She turned away from the spectacular spectacle of beauty in the sky, rolled up the windows of the car with the winding handles one has to crank in a circle; pushed down the elongated knobs one had to press to lock the doors, then closed the car door on the drivers side. She shuffled a small satchel up over her shoulder while jingling the car keys in her hand. She was unintentionally dressed like some hippie. Sparkling bejeweled spaghetti-strap top over a long, flowing, cotton skirt covered in little glittery beads that came to her ankles. Her feet sported leathery sandals that looked like something Jesus or some ancient roman gladiator might have worn. They were in the back of a parking lot; towards the front of the lot it was quite full of parked cars. Next to a wide, short, one-story building that was painted in batches here purple, there green, a pink top with yokelish-blue off side, there was a huge fuchsia-colored blinking neon sign on rooftop that read, "Comedy Mental! Come Get Your Laughs!" In small black letters it said underneath, "Open Wed-Sun 6:PM to 1:AM".

Amii walked the short distance to the back door of the squat building with Miraculum following befuddled behind her. Tugging on the door she discovered it was locked causing in Miraculum an inexplicable urge to bang down the door

with a massive launch of his shoulder.
Amii sighed, Miraculum followed, as the
two of them shimmied their way through
the crowded parking lot on the other side
of the building. The parking lot was
stashed full of cars all the way up to the
walkway near the front door. Amii
lugged open the heavy front door so that
it smashed into Miraculum's face as it
closed on him in a quick thump. He
pulled back and rubbed his nose even
though it didn't hurt. He looked at the
door as if it were foe, shaking a fist at it,
growling. Nevertheless, Miraculum
discovered to his surprise that he was
actually rather quite thrilled to have felt
the mild whomp. Miraculum was keen
of interest as he walked *through* the door
to find a darkened room with a bar to the
back that had a gigantic mirror behind
the various bottles of liqueurs; tables
were full up with humans sitting in
cheesy black plastic chairs. A
multicolored array of round shining bulbs
lit the focal point which was a semi-

circle stage at the back wall of the room. Miraculum saw that Amii stood not far from the door she had just entered.

Amii didn't even realize she had an expression of great bewilderment as she tried looking with immense purpose and intention over the heads of everyone there, in search of someone who looked like they might be the main authority here. The bouncer at the door sized her up, scratched at his ears; he asked Amii, "Do you need help finding a seat?"

"Nope, no, no;" said Amii, "I'm a performer. I'm here to perform." Her head was still held high, her eyes still roving for whom might be in charge of the place. The bouncer, a husky young male in his twenties asked with his eyes widened, "Are you Amii?"

Swiftly Amii turned to the bouncer as her face was all alit, "Yes!" She watched with a rolling nervous energy bumbling around her tummy as the bouncer waved over a fat man with long tangled hair. The bouncer pointed at her several times while mouthing to the tangled haired man the silent name of "Amii" and he wrapped his arms around her shoulders. "You're late;" the bouncer said to her. "I got here as fast as I could," she responded with worry. The rotund man with the gnarled long hair walked over in fast wide steps to quietly place his hand on her back; he pushed Amii in a swoosh to a door which the bouncer opened and the two men ushered her through. Amii with the bouncer pulling, and the gigantesque tangle-hair man pushing, found herself in an extremely dark teeny-tiny hallway, discovering to her dismay that she was being escorted up a short flight of stairs towards the stage. They brought her round to the long back-stage curtains whilst she felt livid looking at the red curtains hanging from the ceiling. Immediately terrified Amii was thinking frantically to herself, 'I can't go on stage yet! I have to prepare! *I'm not prepared*!'

With a pull to her arms the bouncer half whispered to her, "Your on!"

With a swing of his burr-snarly hair the fat man pushed against her back and with the shove Amii found herself standing on the stage with a bright white spotlight beaming down on her. "Ladies and Gentlemen," said a voice booming from somewhere into a microphone, "Amii, The Cosmic Humorist!" The crowd clapped. Clapping is always a reassuring sound. She had been announced! Amii gave a grin with valiant bow. "I am the Cosmic Humorist!"—Amii exclaimed. Everyone clapped. Amii thought, 'Ahhh, clapping, a very good sign.' "Soooo...."—Ami began. Miraculum feeling dejected had sat himself down unseen at a very tiny table at the back corner of the room, where he proceeded to *sulk*.

"Soooo...," said Amii once again, "So. I was a bit shoved onto the stage, but normally I would have a chair on the stage."

"I would have a chair. And this way I could sit down anytime I felt exhausted. Because I have very weak ankles."

"I do. I have very weak ankles, and so I *hate* shopping! I know, your thinking I must be an alien instead of a female if I hate shopping. But I *hate* shopping, because I am forced into complete degradation into using one of those mobile-carts at the grocery store."

"You know the mobile-carts. You know the ones I'm talking about."

"The ones that go very, very, <u>*very*</u> *sssss*lowly. So slow, it's insane! So slow, that your being passed by elderly people with walkers!"

"And they have a long flag attached to them, these shopping mobile-carts. They do, they have a long flag attached to them, you've seen them; don't pretend you haven't been annoyed by them. These things are about six feet tall on a long slim plastic pole, with a bright, *bright* orange flag on the top of it."

"And you know what the bright orange flag on top the thin six-foot plastic pole is *really* for!? It's for temptation! Yeeeeesss, it's for *temptation!*"

"It is. It really is. I'm serious. It's because you're sitting there in your mobile-cart putt-putting along, and you're tempted to grab the thing and pull it back as far as it will go...and then let it go and *THWANG, hit* the elderly person with the walker who is going past you!"

"It is! Because you just have the *urge*, you have the *feeling*, 'How dare you go faster than my mobile-cart!'—It has a battery for goodness sake! So you just have the urge to grab the long thin pole with the bright orange flag on top of it and pull it back as far as it will go…and then the satisfaction of…*THWANG*!—hit the shaking bent-over *smirking* elderly man, right across his head!"

"And you do! You do! And the elderly man just looks a little stunned for a second and totters for a second…"

"…and then **zoom** he's off with his walker, *right past you*!" She paused. "And he's still smirking! The self-pleased elderly little runt! (Another pause.) "Because these flags were *designed* for thwanging upon elderly people… so it really only stuns them for just a *wee* second."

"These flags were also designed so that at Bingo, all the elderly people could laugh and gawk over how many mobile-carts they passed with their walkers. Gives them a sense of satisfaction."

"And the grocery store mobile-cart has this delightful little thing! It's a *delightful* little thing! It has this sound it makes that just sort of scratches down your brain! It's this delightful little thing that when you go in reverse goes, 'Beep Neep Neep!"

"And it *does*! It goes BEEP NEEP NEEP! And the sound just scratches at your **brain**, it does! It's far worse than the proverbial nails down a blackboard…it's just 'BEEP NEEP NEEP!'—and it's like nails…not nails like at the end of your fingertips..but nails like a construction worker might use…just digging, digging, down your… *frontal lobe*!"

"You know what that sounds for, don't you? You know what that's for! It has to go Beep Neep Neep!, because in *reverse* it goes about a *gazillion* times <u>*faster*</u> than it does going *forward*!"

(Applause.)

"It goes so *slow* when your driving the mobile-cart forward, but you put it in reverse and it's like, beeeeeeeeeep-

neeeeeeeep—and your like, "Oh heavens,
I'm moving at the speed of light!" (Puts
hands out in front and turns her head
back.) "Heeeeeeellllllp!! Beep Neep!"

"Now your looking backwards over
your shoulder and waving **whole families**
out of the way! ---Your like thump,
thump, *thump*, 'Oh heavens, there go
the children!' *Smacked the little tykes
right down!*"

(Nervous chuckles. Full laughter. More
applause.)

"You atop your cart. And you're
telling the parents: 'No. He'll be alright.
He's fine! Just pick him up!'"

"The child gets woozily up to his feet
after being run down by your mobile-cart
in reverse, and you're looking at the
parents saying, 'See! He's *standing!*'"

"You wave your hand at the
parents...'See! Standing! *He's perfectly
fine!*'"

"And to your *amazement* the parents are shuffling the child along saying to each other, "He's standing now.' Then they say to their own child, 'You're perfectly *fine*.'"

(Amii holds her hands out helplessly and shakes her head.)

(Miraculum found himself laughing which intensely annoyed him. He would much rather just sit low to grumble sulking.)

Amii the Cosmic Humorist continued: "And I have no choice but to use the stupidly noisy, flag-waving, mobile-cart!"

"I'd rather not!"

"But I've tried it before, just walking around getting my groceries…and suddenly my ankles seize up! I start walking like a *penguin* with their *panties in a bunch*! A sad thing a penguin with their panties in a bunch! And *don't* let

National Geographic fool you...
Penguins *do* wear panties; shiny ones
with sequins! –They just keep them
nicely tucked beneath their feathers.

So then, here I am like..." (—Amii
makes a few steps forward in imitation of
Frankenstein.) "It's no use! I can't
walk any farther. I'm just standing there
doing *nothing*, looking like a complete
dolt!"

"After a while of just standing there,
you find yourself *waving at complete
strangers*." (Amii imitates an
embarrassed expression while waving at
an imagined person passing by.) "You
find yourself saying things like..." —
Amii raises her voice— "I've been
standing here in the same spot for the last
half hour because I *want* to! And then,
very politely you add, How are *you* doing
today?" (Amii imitates an embarrassed
polite smile, waving with one hand,
while holding on to a shopping cart with
the other hand.) "Inexplicably they find

themselves waving back to you! They have no idea who you are, but just in case, they wave back at you anyway. They look at you like you're a mad person; so you know they're walking away thinking, 'That woman is an absolute *dolt*!'"

Amii scratches the side of her nose. "When your using the mobile-cart you should see the way people look at you when it finally gets to be *your* turn at the register to check out!"

"They do things like…"—Amii imitates people looking shocked, covering their mouths; pointing to each other at the person in the mobile-cart with displeased expressions. "Because it's your turn at the register"—Amii presses her lips together in an expression of exasperation—""It's your turn, so you **stand up** out of the mobile-cart."

"People are looking at you like"— Amii again imitates expressions of shock, mouth-covering, and pointing. "Then they start whispering to each other very loudly… 'Oh! Look at that! That woman's been using the mobile-cart this whole time and she can stand! She can stand! Did you see that?'"

Amii rolls her eyes, throws her arms up at her sides then lets them fall with an audible plop against her body. "*Of course* I can stand! What are they thinking? What do they expect?"

"What?! That only paraplegics are allowed to use the mobile-cart?"

"Can't you just see that? A paraplegic rolls into the grocery store in his power-wheelchair, rolls himself up to the mobile-cart, and with *just* the power of his head!….*flings* himself onto the mobile-cart!" (Amii imitates flinging with her head and dangling over the mobile-cart.)

"He's got very powerful strength in just his head, because he's hit the seat of the mobile-cart!"

"But it's just his right *hip* that hits the mobile-cart....because the top of his body is hanging over one side of the cart while his legs and feet are dangling off of the *other* side." (Amii imitates herself as dangling and trying to straighten herself up with just the power of her head. The crowd laughs, moans, claps. She straightens up her body.)

"Or maybe it's that they think only people who are paralyzed from the waist down... can use a mobile-cart."

"So someone who's paralyzed from the waist down, rolls into the grocery store."

"They roll themselves in on their power-wheelchair and up to the mobile-cart, and using just the power of their hands and arms they lift their whole body with phenomenal strength, and still using only the power of their arms they rock themselves side to side, with a count to three….. and one, two, three, they *fling* themselves onto the mobile-cart!…but *no*!...”

“They've missed the whole thing all together, and they're sitting on the floor!”

“That's when they realize that they were unable to hit the seat of the mobile-cart, because they are ***unable to feel their butt***!”

(Amii waits a moment for the laughter and clapping to die down.)

“And I know what you're thinking!”

“I do know what you're thinking!”

“You're thinking, 'Ohhhhh….she's gonna get a bunch of Hate Mail from a bunch of angry people in wheelchairs!”

“But you're wrong!” Amii pointed across the crowd for a moment. “You're wrong! Because many of them have been in my situation at some moment or other in their lives. I have weak ankles!" Amii pointed downward at her legs. "I have weak ankles," she said pointing downward a little lower towards her feet.

"Ohhhhh Kayyyyy…..maybe I *will* get a bunch of Hate Mail from people in wheelchairs. But I will *know* the Hate Mail that comes from paraplegics because even if they have a typewriter their Hate Mail will read something like: z,z,z,q q q rrr, trq, exclamation point, exclamation point, **exclamation point**!" Amii took in a deep breath. "Because they write with their *noses* of course." (She paused.) "When they write… their… Hate Mail."

"I know what you're thinking now!"

"You're thinking, why? Why doesn't she do something about her weak ankles?"

"You're thinking…"—Amii strengthened the tone of her voice very low—"You, you Cosmic Humorist, Amii, you…Why don't you do something about it?" Amii looked out at the crowd smiling. "Well surgery is…"—Amii shook her hands, faining an expression of horror—"…is a bit scary, isn't it."

"So your wondering, well why doesn't she get some pain-killers? Some of you would jump at the chance to legitimately get some pain killers. Wouldn't you? Awww, come one, you know who you are." Amii chuckled and wagged her finger at the crowd.

She took in a deep breath before speaking very solemnly. "I don't get pain killers because pain killers make me think of *Jerry Lewis*."

Amii paused. She smiled while taking in another deep breath. "For those of you who don't recall…Jerry Lewis

was a marvelous, marvelous comedian.
He did a bit with Dean Martin. And
Dean Martin…"—she raised the pitch of
her voice a bit higher—"would play the
part of the straight man, and Jerry Lewis
would…"—she lowered the pitch of her
voice and said with an upper-class
English accent—"play the part of the
very funny man …the very
funny…silly…"—then she acted like she
was searching for a word; then finally
she said extremely fast—"funny man."

"Jerry Lewis hurt his back and started
having to take pain killers. And
something about him changed. Even if
you didn't know what it was, even if you
couldn't put your finger on it, you could
just look at a picture of him, just a
picture of him mind you…and something
inside you would shudder and you'd
think 'something's very wrong with
Jerry these days." Amii sucked in a
breath of air raising one eyebrow in a
quizzical expression. "The French love

him! The French *love* Jerry Lewis!" Amii grinned pausing to siphon air into her lungs, she said as the exhalation of breath came out of her mouth: "Annnnd Nowwww… I'm probably going to get a bunch of Hate Mail from people who are French!"

"Yet I'll be ever so happy as I go through my piles of Hate Mail because I'll be able to pick out the Hate Mail that's from the French and scan through it very quickly, because I'll **know** it right away…"— she lowered the tone of her voice—"…because it will be in *French*."

Amii pretended in the empty air before her to type on a typewriter; frowning hard, she spoke in an extremely angry tone of voice: "Ou` est la cendrier je pouvoir cogne contre votre crane, vous os-tete de porc…pour dire de… *Jerry Lewis*!" Amii grimacing, placed her hands on her hips and faked a spit into the air towards the floor: 'ptoo' is how it sounded as she spat.

"Je courge fromage contre votre visage! Jerry Lewis…le roi…exclamation point, exclamation point, *exclamation point*!" With an angry face Amii spat at the ground again. 'ptoo'!

Then Amii threw her right arm up in the air! She said, "Ladies and Gentlemen you've been a great audience! I thank you very much!" She folded her hands together saying, "And I bid you a good night." Amii bowed gracefully with her hands still in prayer position.

*   *   *

(Amii walked off the stage waving at the crowd quite ridiculously, and grinning at them quite ridiculously as well.) The audience were clapping! Yay!

Barely did Amii have the chance to think to herself, 'They're clapping— that's a good sign', when she was grasped by the arm by a very tall white man whom as he introduced himself ushered her off stage toward the set of short back stage stairs. He had blue eyes, blonde hair, wore a crystal around his neck, and called himself Zeul.

"You were great," he said, "They loved you. I'm one of the performers. Come sit with us, we have our own special table." Zeul guided Amii through the door back out into the theater club. All the comedians and performers were sitting at a large round table that was way far off to the side yet nevertheless directly against the stage. Each person introduced themselves. She remembered their names for a moment until the next person shook her hand. This was frustratingly annoying because now she couldn't just watch the show, she had to listen very carefully to the seated performers conversation in hopes that one would call the other by their name. Her brain happily caught and banked in memory a few names as the night waned.

Amongst the round table were a hue of different looking people in varying shapes and sizes. Next to a man with long curly spirals of black hair that glimmered with a silky sheen, who had toasted warm onyx skin, was sitting another man whom had a handsome full-face with an illustrious sable native American physique. There was an adorable Asian young man after the sable gentleman; seated next to him was a charming man with thick hair, thick flossed eyebrows, whom wore an interesting talisman hung from braided rope around his neck speaking with a Mexican accent. Next to the talisman gentleman were two gorgeous women. One woman spoke with an accent as if she were from India glowing large black eyes with a lustrous rounded hour-glass picturesque robustness. The other woman was unfortunately bone-thin, wearing a risqué black lace sheer cover over a black tank top with pink plaid skirt complementing her fair skin, straight black hair with bangs, and her preciously thick eye-lashed Asian eyes. Amii thought the young Asian man sitting next to the Native American was so fabulously cute she had to resist an urge to run over to him, muss his spiked hair with blue tips by squishing her hand through his locks- saying 'You're so adorable!', then hug him up…hug-hug-hug! Embarrassed suddenly that her face might betray her thoughts to hug him up she turned her attention to the other comedians and wily performers.

She ate bowl after bowl of the free pretzels the waiters brought to the table. Eating them with joy because she was absolutely starving. Amii also drank gleefully the free drinks provided which she suspected were 'watered down'. Amii was only able to drink two shot glass's full of any liquor before she had to wait a full hour to have another one. Otherwise she would get an uncomfortable woozy feeling. Once, she had accidentally gotten drunk on 'Long Island Tea' which didn't taste like alcohol at all; it really did taste like tea, and she ended up spending what felt like an eternity in the women's bathroom at a high class party screaming to her friend: "Please come and save me! And please, please, please make the room stop spinning around!" In her state of mind at that moment in the women's bathroom she really did think her friend could save her by use of some magical power to make the room stop moving in circles. After that unpleasant experience Amii had vowed to be meticulously careful regarding how much alcohol she consumed. Yet here she was sitting with the performers at the comedy club. Within an hour and a half she had drank five margaritas with extra, extra salt around the rim only to simply feel a tiny bit giddy-like floatiness. Yes, the drinks were definitely 'watered down.'

Miraculum joined the table feeling this tad fribbled cheer himself sitting next to the performers in an empty chair directly opposite of where Amii sat. Miraculum watched the stage shows, conjoined with the conversation at the table despite that no-one could see him or hear him.

Closing time came then went and while waiters and bartenders cleaned up, the group of performers alongside Miraculum continued to talk while eating pretzels, sipping their drinks.

"So where are you staying at, Amii?"—asked Zeul.

"Well, I'm just in my car right now," quipped Amii.

"You should see it," said Miraculum grinning as he pointed in a smooth semi-circle at Amii, "it's awful! It's the most beat-up ugly thing I've ever seen!"— Miraculum laughed heartily.

"Okay, I'm off"—said one greasy-haired performer who wore a huge t-shirt, jeans, starring smudgy sneakers on his lopping feet. He got up waving at the others. Everyone including Miraculum waved back.

"Me too;" said another.

"So am I;" spoke the only ventriloquist. Thus the crowd at the table dwindled down to Zeul, Irene, David, Amii, and Miraculum.

"Man," shaking his shoulders, "do you feel a strange presence?"— questioned Zeul of his companeros.

"Yes!" Irene exclaimed with excitement smacking her palms against the table. "Me too! I've felt it too!"

"It's kind of weird you should say that. I felt *something*," David half-mumbled blandly as if bored, in a quite rather resigned tone of voice. He yawned, then scratched at his curly hair abated methodically.

Zeul grabbed the crystal around his neck holding on to it. Zeul and Irene both drew their eyes up to the highest corners as if trying to look at their own brains. The two of them concentrated in thoughtful contemplation to try and 'feel' what this strange presence was.

"The presence is probably *me*!"—shouted Miraculum laughing—"But you're the one that's *strange*!" Miraculum hit the table with his hand whilst laughing harder.

Zeul let go of his crystal, he and Irene locked questioning eyes for a moment. Then Irene, Zeul, and David too, all shrugged their shoulders at the same time in an inadvertent synchronization. Irene and Zeul shook their heads as if conveying to each other that they didn't have a clue. "Well then!"—sputtered Zeul to Amii with a sweeping lift in his

voice—"So you've got no place to stay."
Amii felt a tad bit of embarrassment
flourish heat-tipped in her scarlet cheeks.
She popped a pretzel in her mouth,
chewed, then shook her head 'no'. Zeul
continued to vociferate: "Well then stay
with me at my place! Irene and David
are staying with me. We'll have a good
time."

"That's a great idea;" swooned Irene
as her face lit up with exuberance,
"Come *on*, it'll be fun."

Miraculum placed his strong hand on
Amii's arm, leaned in, whispered in her
ear urgently: "Don't go with them. You
never know who these people are."
Oddly to Amii she felt an immediate
sense of dread that emanated a tactile
possibility of something to fear. It must
have shown on her face. The crowd of
people about her looked puzzled,
expectant. Miraculum snuck closer in to
Amii once more placing his voluminous
hand on her fragile arm, whispering like

a feathery wind: "Tell you what, go ahead and go with them. I'll keep an eye on these people for you." All at once Amii felt a vigorously strong feeling of calm waft over her like a cool autumn breeze. Indeed it seemed alright to go with these strangers to their house.

"Come on;" struck up Zeul, "Don't be scared. One more is no problem; I've got plenty of room."

David spoke softly in sequel yawn with languid return to scratch his curly-haired head once more: "We're good people."

"Very good," affirmed Irene, nodding her chin while a serene closed-lip smile blossomed upon her mouth.

"Okay," Amii shrugged her shoulders, stood up from her chair returning the pleasured beam of face-shine to Irene. "I'm parked in back."

"We'll be the only blue van in the parking lot. Just follow us." Irene stood up. "We'll pull the *blue* van in the back for you. All you have to do is follow us. We'll try not to go through any yellow lights on you so that you're stuck at a red one. Ha!" Irene winked and patted Amii's shoulder, then reiterated, "Just follow us."

Miraculum and Amii were about to walk unwittingly into a most *surprising* unknown.

SEVEN

The manager-owner of the comedy theater walked up to the final lingering group. "Hey! I'm the manager...*and* I own the place!"- she said to Amii with well-earned pride- "Everyone pose!" She held in her dark ebony skin hands an old Polaroid instant film camera, with her shiny black face grinning she placed the lens against her eye to look through the little camera window snapping the instant shot. "I'll make one for each of you, and one for the club board." Irene, David, Zeul, Amii, and Miraculum all grouped together, the humans placing their arms around each other smiling, while Miraculum inexplicably made the

'peace' sign with both of his hands…
smiling open-mouthed like a happy
drunkard, as he stood right behind Amii.
"Here," said the manager as she handed
one picture that came out of the camera
with a buzzz-zzzt sound to Zeul. Then
another buzzz-zzzt snap shot which she
handed to Amii, another for Irene,
another for David, then a buzz pop of one
more for posterity to pin up on the large
board covered already in pictures just at
the entrance of the club. Everyone
smiled and a few triumphed 'Yay' or
'Hooray'. They shook their thick photos
while blowing breath on them, waiting
for the image to develop in magic-like
appearance. Grinning, the manager
named Margie marched over to the
board. She stuck the picture still
underdeveloped onto it with a stick pin.
Miraculum followed her watching. As
Margie walked away he felt a new
strange thing called 'sadness' as he
fingered the picture quite forlornly
feeling the picture should have belonged

to *him*. The others would look at their
pictures much later in time to muse over
the mixture of shadow and light in the
background that appeared as one looked
upon it as though someone foggy were
standing in the background holding up
'peace' signs with their hands. No-one
took the time to wait for the image
development of their pictures at this time
due to a sempiternal appreciation that
they were hurried to get out of the club.
Thus they tucked their pictures in
pockets, purses, satchels, to look at a
great time later with selvage impressions
of spooky marvel. Thusly, only
Miraculum saw the developed picture as
he stared peckishly chagrined at the
board. He saw with rapturous excitement
that a blurry, shiny, white-orange image
of himself showed up behind the
performers like a ghostly apparition yet
the 'peace' signs of his hands were
unmistakable. This gave him some lofty
satisfaction.

"I'll walk you to your car", said the manager Margie to Amii, "I've parked in the back as well." Margie must have overheard some of their conversation. Amii agreed with silent affirmation so that everyone, including Miraculum, shuffled out the front door waiting respectfully for the manager-owner to lock it tight against vandals or hooligans possibly tempted to invade the liquor bar or spray-paint the already circus veined spectacle of the walls. The money-safe was so thoroughly hidden tucked down away beneath floorboards then foam-rubber, carpeted, topped off with file cabinet heavy laden that no-one would ever find it for a thousand years until some tired bored archeologists came picking, brushing, piddling to unearth the remnants of a vast past civilization; at which point the money would become one of two extremes. Either worth a great deal or nothing at all. Margie turned the last bolt in its upright and locked position then turned with a beautiful toothy smile placing her hand upon Amii's back as if to be the sole director towards the back parking lot. Miraculum hopped along behind them with peccantly errant thoughts of prophetic curiosities fluttering around his mind as he pondered the nature of the bizarre adventure he seemed to be having.

"Just remember. Follow us.;" Irene hollered to Amii. "We'll be in the blue van!"

"It's right there!"—Zeul spoke, as he and David both pointed at the boxy blue van while the group of them marched out into the parking lot that still emanated vents of heat from the concrete.

Margie, Amii, and Miraculum strolled amongst the neon lit comedy sign flashes past the street light around the corner to the back of the building. Here Margie's car was not parked far from Amii's sunbird. "I'm so glad you came tonight

said the owner handing Amii cash
money. Without counting it Amii
opened her satchel stuffing the cash
inside, yet before she could zip up her
hippie looking purse the manager and
Amii oddly looked up at the same time,
having felt the unknown presence slink
into their auras to disturb their personal
bubbles of energy. The two women
looked up simultaneously to see a skinny,
scrubby, fairly short man in tattered
clothing whom had come around from
the other end of the building which was a
darkened, disturbingly caliginous gloom
of tenebrous non-illuminated swarth,
running up to them at an alarming rate!
The man approached them voraciously
directly, so much as to raise ones hackles
then hex ones lungs to forcibly inflate
with air. The streetlamp shining down its
loyal kindle revealed in the
incandescence the glint of a small knife
in the man's hand! Although the tatter-
clothed shabby man with ancient dirt
smears everywhere on his thin skin was

shorter than Margie (just nearly to Amii's five-foot three-inch height) he was with the gleaming little blade quite a set for forbidding warning. He was jittery shaking, continually scratching painfully hard at his scalp with his left hand. The grimy fellow couldn't seem to stand still. His squinty eyes kept blinking then zooming in a searching manner from one side to the other far too fast and much too often.

The women stood like statues; their minds electrified blank. Miraculum felt a surge of powerful protectiveness along with a new feeling he had never quite understood called 'fear.' He also felt something oddly new called 'apprehension.' With manly determination Miraculum ran full strength leaping to enter Amii's body. He slammed his head against hers, bumping his body smack-dab against her body. He bounced backwards so viciously hard that he actually did a

back-flip then skidded back a few feet
upon the ground on his bottom.
Miraculum had forgot. He can not enter
Amii. Amii slung her head in her hands,
squeezing her eyes shut in a sudden
violent pain, --"Ow!"—she screamed,
"OH! My head! OH! Ahhh! I think I'm
getting a migraine!"

The manager Margie put a hand on
Amii in instant concern, "Are you
alright!?," she exclaimed. Then her eyes
darted back upon the jittery, scalp-
digging, squinty man who chewed his
lips with yellow broken teeth as he
maintained holding the knife in flustered
foaming gutter stutter, "C..c..come on!
Come on! Give me your purse! Give me
your purse!" Then he squinted
exceptionally menacingly hard at the
manager in his inability to stand still
demanding, "And you, *you*, give me your
money! Give me your money!"

The blinding white light of pain was
all that Amii could see in her head as it

catapulted her back to an exigent banished pouf of pitiful nutty memory that had the reminiscence of ignoble importance; although what express significance escaped her. A childhood recollection which she experienced now as if she were actually truly there both reliving it while watching it at the same time. Amii saw herself as she was pulled along by her mother's grasp into grade-school down the hallway to where the art-teacher stood enjoying looking at the pictures her young pupils had drawn that she'd proudly taped to the wall for all the parents and other students to see. The mother marched up to the art teacher, "You asked me to come in?"—said the mother with a cold stern no funny-business tone. "Yes," the art teacher replied looking down at the small frightened eight year old Amii who didn't know what was going on. The art teacher flipped her thin brown hair back over her ear, took from her right hand a large picture which she unrolled; it was a beautiful meticulously drawn pencil drawing Amii had created of ancient Jerusalem. "Your daughter has great talent. Look at this. It's so impressive!" Then blew a strand of her brown hair out of her eyes carelessly letting the large picture roll back up as she let go of it with one hand. The teacher spoke: "But every time I ask the children to draw pictures of people, there are no mouths and no hands on any of the people Amii draws." She pointed and continued: "Look at this!"—the teacher tapped Amii's notebook sized picture on the wall—"I asked the children to draw a picture of their family. This is Amii's picture. Everyone are very far apart, and stiff; none of them have mouths. And see… everyone's arms are hid behind them so that there are no hands." Pausing for inflection of silent seriousness the teacher looked from mother to child before continuing: "I'm concerned. I got my minor in psychology and these pictures of people

are very concerning. I think your
daughter needs some counseling. I think
she would do well to receive some
professional therapy." The mother bent
over hugely demanding across little
Amii's body, commanding the
demarcation of the child, "Why don't
you draw hands?! Tell the teacher why
you don't draw hands!" Fearful of the
situation and of what might happen when
they got home, Amii thought nervously
fast for an answer; then looking at the
teacher said as casually and flippant as
she could muster, "I just can't draw
hands well." With this Amii wrung her
hands together in reddened tightness
looking down at the floor. Proclaimed
the mother: "There! She just can't draw
hands well!" Then with sparking
intention the mother put her eyes so close
to the art teachers eyes that there was
barely an inch between them; which
brought forth fear in the art teachers
eyes. With a calm yet angry protective
viciousness the mother said, "Don't tell

me what to do with my child. Don't tell *me* what my child needs." It seemed a delusive demonstration of prosaic protection on the mother's part, when she swung around grabbing her child's hand to pull Amii away; but as she watched the memory of her mother pulling her away the entire background of the school faded into nothing but white light. Then Amii heard a man's low gentle voice urging her: "Come to Nnema! Come to Nnema! Take Nnema's hand." Looking to her right and upwards she saw a man surrounded by the white light whom wore a robe, looking like a wizard from some fairy-tale. Flinging her arm out straight Amii grabbed hold of his outstretched hand; he yanked her so hard into the blinding white light that she was instantly popped right back in her body. Still holding her head with one hand during the few passing moments, the pain receding, an expression of discomforting confusion on her face, she opened one eye, peeking at the jittery smudgy man wielding the small glinting knife biting his lips with his yellow broken teeth.

Miraculum had a severe dogged unrelenting expression on his face as he sprung up off his butt running rush full force at the club manager. Miraculum *shoved his arm into Margie the managers arm* and with a ridiculously strong hit he cold-cocked the jittery thief with his fist straight up the man's nose.

The man was thrown back falling on *his* butt. Then he crawled backward like a crab pulling himself to his feet as a trickle of blood rolled out of one nostril. He dropped the knife on the ground to walk backward, backward, *and backward*, until he was once again at the dark corner of the building where he immediately turned and ran away.

"Wow!"—exclaimed Margie looking at her fist—"I had no idea I could do that!" Miraculum slid his arm out of Margie's arm whereby it fell quickly limp at her side. She lifted her hand, wriggled her fingers while eyeing her knuckles then exclaimed once more, "Wow!'

The blue van screeched up near to them. Irene gestured with a beckoning motion as the square doors at the back of the van flung open by David and Zeul, while all of them were calling, "Get in! Get in! Hurry up! Get in!"

The manager retrieved her car keys from her pocket then shakily jammed the car key into the lock with swift tour de force of loose clicking in the closure letting go. She swung herself inside, closed the door in a frightened flurry, pushing down the elongated knob with one numb finger so that the door was locked lickety-split once again. She peered wide-eyed and impressed out the tinted window as she absently shoved the key into the ignition. Starting the car her foot dropped heavy on the gas revving the engine.

Amii and Miraculum ran at the blue van, jumped hearts beating wild, into the back. Several of Miraculum's quills fell fluidly as fecundate shooting feldspar. A waft of forfeited feathers. David and Zeul closed the large lofty boxy doors at the back of the van with an urgent heave. Zeul locked it. Irene began driving the van out of the parking lot into the hazy, golden, half-harvest moon sky of lazy night-time streets.

"Holy cow, man! What was that all about?"—asked David with an interestingly pleased grin on his face.

"Oh my gosh!"—hooted Zeul.

"I think we were being robbed," said Amii blandly.

"You think?,"—laughed David.

"Man! We totally saved you!"—whooped Zeul once again in the adrenaline excitement. Then Zeul and

David 'high-fived' each other in a smarting smack of their palms.

"We're gonna have fun tonight guys," shouted Irene over her shoulder as she drove the blue archaic van, "I wanna go swimming!"

Amii was rubbing her forehead. Zeul asked with genuine concern, "What's wrong?"

"I've got a headache."

"Here." David fluffed his hand through his leather-fringed man-purse retrieving three pills. "Take these."

"What are they?" Amii glanced at the pills dubiously.

"This one," David pointed out, "is valium. These two are aspirin." He was telling the truth.

Shrugging her shoulders wishing an end to the menacing headache Amii grasped hold of all three pills popping them in her mouth. She wrinkled up her face for the pills were so sour they practically pulsated on the back taste-buds of her tongue. Eyes darting, she began looking around frantically for something liquid to swallow them with. Her throat was stolidly gaunt against allowing the pills to slide through her esophagus because of the high-fire warning of contemptuous bitterness. Supremely transcending the malady of acrid rancorous flavor soaking now into the back part of her tongue would be like purposely taking in air while diving without a snorkel. Her squinched scowling recoil of expression was an alert which received response.

"Oh!"—sensed David so that he thrust his hand underneath the front seat producing a bottle of warmed water that had been rolling around; he handed it to Amii. Taking it quickly from him she unscrewed the cap, with one eye open and the other eye clenched she hurriedly

drank deeply. Saying 'Ahhh' afterward
to her throats relief from the half-melted
jagged pills with abysmal acrimonious
nightshade flavor. Wiping her mouth
with the back of her hand, she rubbed the
loosening grip of ache off her forehead.
Letting the rides cooling night shadows
seep past them in the drive quenched her
worries alleviating tension. Streetlamps
next to shiny pastel neon lights from
establishments sliding in and out of the
windows during the pleasantly
comfortably completely silent drive,
Amii alongside the others were moon-lit
lunar, transcendent by the quiet. The trip
seemed quickly cheerful in the lovely
mute hush.

Arriving at Zeul's house Amii was
delightfully surprised to see that the
abode was quite big with luscious clean-
blue swimming pool in the moon-
drenched backyard. Puffy multicolored
floaties of blue, red, white and yellow
proposed Amii's favorite clear-watered

chlorine-scented pleasure, which was to float on the plastic pumped up pool toys with complaisant splashing happiness. All the better that Zeul's pool was preciously bath-water warm! Amii splish-splashed her fingers in the soothing warm waters whilst looking up into the night sky loftily gleaming a moon with precipitous red rings around it in the sifting clouds. Zeul played music he called heavy-metal that had sweet enduring words of spirit strength, all of which was new to both Amii and Miraculum. Miraculum temporarily animated his night-bloom shaded wings to appear dipping them into sun-warmed water as he floated on the pool's acute tepid liquid with joyful benefit of a floaty. Hands beneath his head, his body bobbing next to Amii. She saw the celestial stars blinking in the heavens upon the earnest earthy backdrop of the ebon sky above. Concentrating on one empyrean ethereal body that twinkled several colors nearly fainting her with its beauty. "It used to be my mother's house," Zeul explained, as everyone went quietly joyfully swimming in the pool (Miraculum included of course.) Miraculum and Amii were splashing themselves around the water with swishes of their hands, gazing gratefully at the beauty of the starry, starry night's effervescent moon gleaming above them like shining diamonds. Although no-one could see Miraculum not a one thought anything of the empty pool-float he lay upon whilst nevertheless moving it around in the water for the sheer fun of the ripples. Everyone assumed the floaty's movement was the result of the light warm breeze blowing, therefore gave it not the least attention. Miraculum gazing at the night sky yearned for his Home and his Family in his heaven as he ravished in the star-filled great wide open above him.

Once all present had their fill of swimming they raided the refrigerator in famished plunder. Bagels smeared with cream-cheese, apricot preserves, and olives were devoured with delectable delight. Whilst Miraculum watched them gleefully munch on the food he felt an envy of dejection that he could not also nosh and dine. He had unanimated his wingspan to pull them inward to the energy of his stippled vertebrae; sorrowfully watching the humans as he sat on the kitchen barstool. He sulked. Having their consuming fill it then seemed to the humans a wonderful idea to go out on the front patio thus soaking in the magnificent nightly sky some more; an idea which perked Miraculum up a bit. The front patio was lain of reddish bricks with a very short bricked wall all around except where it ended at an opening looking out upon the driveway. Irene relaxed all the way back in a lounge chair. Zeul sat next to her holding her delicate hand, his head resting with the back of his neck against her leg; the brick patio beneath him still slightly warm from the days soaking in of sunlight. David sat on top of the short red brick wall seeming happy to admire the heavenly expanses. Amii turned to notice for the first time since she'd arrived a long ladder leaning from the floor of the patio all the way up to the top of the flat one-story Spanish-tile roof. David turned his head with the intuitive sense of movement behind him, watching with interest as Amii ascended the ladder. Following along, for it seemed like a good idea, David and Miraculum climbed the ladder after Amii to the roof of Spanish-tile.

Amii stood in the *center* of the roof out of some odd and untouchable fear that she might inexplicably toddle right off the edge of it for absolutely no reason at all save for an impossible bizarrely unfortunate flux in the laws of gravity. She knew this was nonsense yet submitted to her tingling apprehension. David stood approximately four feet away from her, yawning, smiling, and tossing his curly hair. Miraculum sat down in the roof's center near Amii to cross his legs one over the other. *Then a most unusual event took place*!

As David, Amii, and Miraculum looked up at the black noir sky before them they noticed three bright lights in the sky forming a triangle! Then the three lights zoomed faster than anything any human military has ever yet invented or let known so that they were in a blink all side by side to the far left. Then four more bright lights appeared above the first three and in a not-yet-invented (or known) blink they were on the far right of the sky in the formation of a star with two dots in the middle.

Then in a 'not yet invented' by any scientist or military way, the seven bright lights zoomed in an amazingly fast blink to the center of the sky; where they formed a complete circle with one light in the center of the circle! Lachrymose looming levitating featherweight illumination in unidentifiable manifest exhibition idled, darted, sailed in a sweep of the macrocosmos via limitless lightning speed!

"That's not normal;" stated Amii in a low, slow, shocked voice.

"That's not normal at all"—stated David in the same engulfed goggle of shock.

Then the circle of lights zoomed/appeared to the far left of the dark sky blinking in different unmistakable shimmering colors of red, blue, green, and white.

Began Amii: "Oh...my..."

"Buddha" : David finished her sentence.

"Buddha?," asked Amii amused; she laughed. They were both completely insatiably unable to take their eyes off of the bespectacled sight. (Miraculum was gazing with the same amazement.)

All at once every huge light turned white and parted *instantaneously!* Now there were three on the far left, three on the far right, and one in the very middle. Their movement only took a second!

Their eyes still glued to the sight, Amii asked, "Is there some sort of military testing around here?" Her mind was racing for an understandable fully answering explanation.

"Yes," answered David very slowly, without looking away from the phenomena.

"Have you ever known or heard of any military aircraft that can move like that? That instantaneously?" Her eyes were glued to the paradox of wonder taking place.

Miraculum was jumping up and down with excitement. "What's a military

aircraft?! What's a military aircraft?!"
He was bouncing with saltate springing
exhilaration all atwitter.

"No;" David answered Amii's
question unwavering from the view still
awash brimful of reverence and
stupefaction.

Effete lights in the expanse of welkin
space surrounding up-above expanded
out into a skillful broad round
circumference as a perfect circle except
for the one in the center which came
closer. Closer. *Closer* still without
desisting; with expeditive break-neck
speed, so that Amii, Miraculum, and
David all watching found themselves
uncontrollably stepping backwards!
Posthaste!-Pronto!-The craft flew down
descending towards them quick as
lightning as if the thing might crash right
on top of them! It quickly flew directly
over them on the roof they were standing
upon; all three of them without even
meaning to instinctively ducked down.

Dodging their bodies downward while gazing upward dumbfounded and aghast with surprise all three of them incidentally without even meaning too said the exact same words at the exact same time…"What the…," and they all said the 'F' word.

The craft came so mesmerizingly close that it looked as if you could literally reach up and touch it! The thing seemed to hover for a moment. Many lights shining underneath it, one could get a good look at the thing, it truly seemed to be at the very least a mile or more wide! So large was the craft that it was hugely, completely, engulfing! All on the roof got a good long drink of an eyeful. Everyone began to stand up from their crouching position. Standing and looking up astounded. Then as meticulously surely fixed as it was the craft with it's barely audible hum (if there was a hum at all, for they might have simply been feeling the breeze); a

moaning in fact that was so nearly silent
it might well have been created from the
caressing air around them suddenly
zoomed with such harefooted alerted
swiftness that all present stood spine
straight and gawked at the instant shot as
their eyes followed it swarm far up into
the sky! The distinct object shined bright
in tantalizing worshipful tempo of
temporary suspension! Adhered eyes
upon the entity ushered supplant when
the flying doodad nimbly fleeted in a
flushed flurry to the far right of the sky!
Then it zipped upward, fantastically fast,
in the blink of an eye, with this sprightly
zing the object simply disappeared.
Blank black Zion left in the sky, now
empty, where the huge glowing thing had
just immediately been!

Taking a moment to waver out of the
sheer awe of the occurrence, Miraculum,
David, and Amii finally realized that
Zeul and Irene were shouting while
jumping up and down in their thrilled

screams from down below on the patio. Miraculum, David, and Amii, all ran without a thought of fear of heights directly to the edge of the roof to look down. Irene and Zeul were flabbergasted with excitement; hopping into the air repeatedly…up and down…up and down…as they both glared expectantly towards the Spanish tile rooftop shouting up at their comrades: "Did you see that?! *Did you see that*?!" Of course the gelid artful craft gargantuan of prophetic sizes could not help but be seen! Yet a witness to such majestic phantasms makes the heart less heavy to those who have seen. "Did you SEE that?!!"—Irene and Zeul announced to their roof-bound friends.

"Yes! I saw it! Did you see that!?" David was also asking Irene and Zeul if they too had seen the thing. The air filled with exalts of 'Yes! Yes!' all around so that everyone felt reassured.

"It was incredible!"—Miraculum shouted down to Zeul and Irene even

though they could not see nor hear him—
"What was that?" Miraculum was just as
excited with the drum of adrenocortical
thrill as he whooped out loud. "It was
beautiful!" He would have unleashed the
very atoms that released at will the
projected expansion of his gusty
feathered appendages flying about in a
thrill, but like a child who refuses to go
to bed at his bedtime he was too
interested in what the humans were
saying and doing and did not want to
miss out on any winking word or action.
"I can fly if I want too!"—he yelled
baritone voiced downward to the
unhearing people on the patio—"I can fly
too!" He was like the extra small child
that the older children try to ditch.
Miraculum ached to prove that he too
could be exciting plus (in his kind's
perception at the very least) beautiful!
"What was that thing!?"—Miraculum
shouted to Zeul.

"It was so close, we ducked down!"— hollered Amii.

David was continuing the affirmation in exclamation as he felt the full flowing tingling. "Yeah, we did too! We totally ducked down!"

Miraculum bent down placing his hands on the edge of the roof to yell out: "I ducked down too!" He was feeling both excited and left out at the same time.

Amii, Miraculum, and David, all climbed down the ladder so that the whole group congregated next in the living room of the house. Zeul put on some soft, gentle, soothing music with whale calls in it. All present began settling down in the living room to rest. It was unspoken acceptance that nobody wished to be away from anyone else while trying to sleep after such odd and magnificent oeuvre nocturnal occurrence. Irene on the couch, David in the lounge-

chair, Zeul on the chaise, Amii on the
floor with a knitted afghan she'd found
then pulled over herself with a small
couch pillow beneath her head.
Miraculum shafted his wings to reappear
from the energy enclosure that would be
his spine for his pleasure and his
comfort. He rested high above them all
with his back feathers against the ceiling;
his arms folded flat upon the ceiling
behind his head.

EIGHT

Thus Miraculum rested with his body flattened against the cream-colored corrugated ceiling, his knuckles bearing into the roughness beneath his head, where he could peep an eye at any of the humans sleeping below if he so desired. It took him a long time for his mind to flow into the meditative state, like so many insomniacs who exhaust themselves trying hard to force themselves to fall asleep. For his mind was bereft with wondering ponderings and meanderings... 'What is a military aircraft?'... 'Why can't I eat bagels and cream-cheese?'... 'What is going on!?' 'Poor, poor Miraculum', he thought suffering to himself. For his mind was exigently exhumed mesmeric deep in confusion.

Every human fell in to the depths of sleep. Amii drifted into a dream whereby she was walking through a gorgeous antiquated village neighborhood where snow was falling. Trees were full-up with colorful autumn hues of red, magenta, and flaming burnt-orange. Snow covering everything left a ground thickly shiny with the crystalline sparkles. Children amidst their families were playing in the powdery snow wearing winter clothes, throwing snowballs, sledding, waving back to Amii as she passed them. Then she came to a yard which in the dream she knew to be her personal own. In this yard was a large most perfectly shaped snowman that had zero adornments save but two dark rock eyes in it's face with two equally gray rock ears that were stubbed into the sides of it's snowman head to appear nearly as shadowy slits. At once

Amii realized there were no more people, the neighborhood deserted. She still looked around to see no-one, even though she already knew she was alone, a feverishly futile stolid attempt. Emotional senses awry with the numb prudent discernment that something was terribly wrong filled her up to capacity. She walked over to the front of the snowman in her yard. Something ruby and sticky began to seep out of it's shady-gray rock eyes and ears. A slow second passed when without hesitation gushes of bright red blood began to *pour* out of the snowman's eyes and ears! It kept pouring rushing out; scarlet crimson pooling in gooey circles upon the snow white ground. Horror sloshed through Amii's dream-spirit from her feet to her face to compound in an alarmed expression of astonishment. Fear zinged a signal of being overwhelmed! Amii screamed! From somewhere around her like a spinning breeze she heard, "Come to Nnema." It was as if the words circled

around her with the wind! She searched
for this person 'Nnema' but could not see
him. Turning in a circle she scanned the
area frantically with her grieving eyes, as
she screamed and *screamed* for him, the
disembodied male rumble low waltzing
voice that beckoned her. Rising throws
of distress overflowed to unbearable
levels ..."Nnema!"—Amii shrieked—
"Nnema! Nnema!" Suddenly in startling
immediate appearance the old man in the
long robe named Nnema who looked like
some fairy-tale wizard floated down, one
foot in front of the other as if he were
about to land! Yet he snatched Amii up
with eloquent speed, wrapping his arms
tight around her, pulling her up and out
of the dream. She was in Nnema's arms
rapidly transported into Zeul's living
room where she could look down to see
her own sleeping body. Nnema flew
down very close to her body and actually
tossed her into it! She felt like she'd
rolled into her body with the tug of an
inescapable water's tide. Amii's body

sat bolt upright with her eyes open but not yet seeing, she heard herself loudly screaming bloody horror. Amii's scream was so violent and prolonged that it woke everyone up. Miraculum's soft wide-span of beautiful dark wings disappeared with a sound like a zipper being closed very quickly.

Miraculum whom had been non-asleep eyes closed in meditative silence found to his unstoppable laurels that without his control, his arms and legs swung out in the startled stiff shape of an 'X'. It was as if gravity that had forgotten him, suddenly remembered him at once! Miraculum's eyes popped open as he waved his arms wildly; he fell from the ceiling landing smack-dab on his face when he hit the floor with a wallop! The superb surprise did not surpass him and he didn't know whether to laugh or to be angry. So he turned his face sideways *thus removing his nose from its smashed position crunched into the carpet.* In his lack of decision for what to feel, either humored or infuriated, he simply lay there breathing moaning. At last a chortled chuckle hiccupped from his mouth, but he still lay flagrantly flat.

Everyone had scurried awake in the whiz-bang scream. Irene rushed off the couch in a half-crawl grabbing Amii's hands. Amii huffed air rapidly as she at once saw Irene's face. Her hard breathing settling slowly as she looked at Irene while blinking her dreary eyes in the dripping sweat from her face. Irene held fast to Amii's hands. she looked directly into Amii's eyes with searching concern, "Was it? I mean. Did the UFO's scare you?" Amii made the noise of 'Nnn-nnn' and shook her head 'no.' "A bad dream?'—Irene asked. Now Amii made the noise of 'Mmm-Hmm' shaking her head 'yes.' "Ohhhhh," murmured Irene softly, gently wrapping her arms around Amii in the sweetest, unconditionally loving, hug that Amii had ever felt. Zeul and David gathered close so that the four of them formed a tight circle; one by one they each hugged Amii with an unconditional intent of tenderness the likes of which she had *never* known before. The hugs had a feeling to them that she could palpably feel as pure *unconditional* love, serenely deep these hugs touched a part of her soul that seemed familiar, yet indescribable. She *knew* that feeling from somewhere. Like a blossoming Calla-Lilly with it's huge one petal pale purple-white blossom damp with dew; or a ripe Sunflower the size of a gigantic disc gleaming fluorescently sun-soaked yellow; the sensation was so majestically mystically familiar. It was morning now, the night gone with the hue of sunrise, the sun peeked in slants through the windows. Amii gratefully simplistically melted like warmed butter into each hug as if it were a gold-spun sari draped around her, to savor the sweet pure feeling.

Miraculum lay doggedly defiant staying flattened on the floor. Apparently he'd 'slept' through the whole thing in moaning nonplussed amusement when Irene's friends (Molly and Sara) came brashly barging through the unlocked front door. His eyes popped open from their half-moon crevice. Discovering himself jumping to his feet, hollering sarcastically , "Oh great! Now who are *these* people!?"

"We're going out to the caves! There's an old mining ghost town there, a real one, but they've reopened the shops...I've been wanting to go there for ages! Up! Up! I've made sandwiches for everyone!"—Sara stated this announcement very loudly. (Her hearing was not quite so good.) Sara and Molly stood holding hands looking young and absolutely adorable. Like two people whom had found a true secure love. Molly with her thick curly hair, wearing boots, shorts, and a t-shirt, had a fresh scrubbed face. Sara blinked at Amii with the wide-eyed child-like realization that there was someone new in the room. "Why don't *you* come with us too? What's your name?"

"Amii."

"Molly, can Amii come with us too? It's okay, right?"

Molly softly mussed a few thick curls on her head, then rested her hand on her cheek for a moment. "Sure. Why not. We're goin' to the caves with the ghost town; wanna join us?"

Amii looked at the others with an equally wide-eyed, child-like, sense of wonder then with a shrug said, "Sure!"

Pulling a long strand of her sandy colored hair from her face Sara said, "Yay!," she kissed Molly on the cheek.

No-one else wanted to go, claiming they ached and were all much too tired. But the adrenaline of Amii's dream had her buzzingly wide awake; not to mention the whole event sounded like a fun adventure. This was as it turns out, much to Miraculum's relief. He truly wanted to go too! He wanted to see the cave, and the word 'ghost' in ghost-town especially appealed to him. Miraculum was relieved because he did not want to test his boundaries of how far away from Amii he could go without being pulled back.

"Alrighty then," said Sara as she let go of Molly's hand to head for the door, "I'll be right back."

"Where are you going?"—inquired Molly.

"To get the sandwiches. I'll be right back." She exited and returned in a moment with a large paper sack. Sara handed out a thoroughly appreciated sandwich to Irene, David, and Zeul, then she grabbed Molly's hand urging Amii forward to follow with a few beseeching swings of the large paper sack.

"We'll be back around evening," informed Molly. Thusly Molly, Sara, Amii and Miraculum all left the house with Miraculum slamming the door shut causing everyone to slightly jump, glare at the door, behemothly silently blaming the wind.

Molly, Sara, Amii, and Miraculum climbed into the silver four-door car, with Miraculum and Amii of course in the backseat. All present put on their seatbelts, including Miraculum who had absolutely no idea why they were doing such a thing, he simply didn't want to be any different than the others. Amii heard an extra 'click'. She looked over at the empty seat next to her. She had been certain the seatbelt had been open and unlocked when she'd gotten into the car. Wide open eyes as she stared at it, the seatbelt was locked and closed in the seat next to her. Amii thought this odd for a creepy fleeting moment then she shook off the feeling, simply assuming she had been wrong. Molly began driving whilst Sara dug through the large paper sack. She handed an egg-salad sandwich to Molly then handed one back to Amii. She sat one for herself on her lap. She looked into the bag with consternation saying, "If you want more there's plenty. I've got five extra ones in the bag." Sara looked over at Molly. "Do you think I should have given more to the others? I didn't even think about it."

"No, no," Molly reassured Sara, "You did just fine."

Amii thanked them both for the sandwich. Miraculum attempted to reanimate his wings, which took great effort as if trying to move a boulder! His face reddened as he bore down tightening his body, when at last they pressurize-poofed out in a flittering fluff of feathers that swirled then floated down through the air! A splash of quills that he wished

Amii could see had removed themselves without his will! His wings crunched up behind him; the auditory reverberation they made when they had opened was like an airbag deploying from somewhere off in the distance while at the same time honking a sound that was like an amateur child experimenting a blow of air through a trumpet... *'BLATT!'* This volute sonance peaked the expression on Amii's face emanating her vulnerable to the ostentatious offensive voluminosity that was involuntary...*did that sound come from her*? Embarrassment dominated her nerves in a physical heat that rose from her stomach past her countenance to her ears. Even the roots of her hair seemed hot and tingly. For lack of what else to do Amii leaned forward a little bit saying: "Umm...excuse me?" Molly mumbled 'not to worry about it' rolling her car-window down a crack. Sara who kept a small can of air-freshener in the glove compartment, opened the glove-compartment, pulled out the little can, stretched her arm into the backseat and sprayed. Wet streams of damp gardenias infiltrated the backseat with it's strong scent. Amii closed her eyes against the spritz of airborne flowery liquid while it settled. Of course it was Miraculum who had made the sound, yet no-one knew this! Most disconcerting was that Amii was left to think she had discovered an entire new knowledge in her life that one could possibly pass *gas* without knowing it was coming and without feeling it come out! She thought this an abhorrently painful realization!

Since Amii believed that if you can't say something nice then try for pity sake not to say anything at all, she determined to stay silent while eating her sandwich; after all what 'nice' thing could one possibly converse about regarding such a sound? Then she decided to *thank them again for the food*; she had already said 'excuse me', thus this act seemed

pleasingly final. Amii ate the sandwich
with delicious relishing. It smelled of
yeasty fresh bread and lemons. On her
taste buds she detected amidst the
smooth creaminess an odd shaped
crunchiness with flavors of paprika and a
pinch of sage. Miraculum watched Amii
eating. He also wanted an egg-salad
sandwich, thus feeling left out
Miraculum folded his arms, with a scowl
on his face, *and sulked.*

The car ride seemed quick, perhaps
due to excitement. They all explored the
cave first. Wet and dark, cool to the
skin; full of crystals. Then they delved
into investigation for the possibilities of
interest in the 'ghost town'; a wild west
display with an old mine for diamonds or
gold or some such treasure, hailing
wayward railway tracks; dusty banter
saloon doors of creaky wood.
(Miraculum was faintly disappointed that
they didn't find any real ghosts.) To the
end of their adventurous quarry they at

last walked up to the top of a tall hill that rounded past the old timey shops and sported a huge red-clay colored boulder. Miraculum spread out to look up at the sky; he felt happy. His hands beneath his head, booted feet crossed at the ankles, wings swimming in the heat at his spine; he had his lateral petals out the entire time for fear that it might take an unpleasant amount of effort to reanimate them. This was the first experience Miraculum ever knew that made him question his right to look however he wanted; his wingy fleets were more important to him than he'd ever realized.

"What do you want to do now?"—asked Molly of Amii.

"What I want is rain!"—exclaimed Amii joyfully. "I *love* a good thunderstorm! With a warm rain, that is, if your going to be out in it. I wish it would rain."

"Izah' clear sky," said Molly. "Reckon' you'll have ta' wait, Amii. Too bad too really, we could use some rain." She pecked a little kiss on Sara's cheek then looked up at the sky. "Yep. We could use some rain. Not a cloud in the sky. Too bad."

Hopping onto the boulder with a straddle of her arms and legs, Amii joked: "Well, I'll just make it rain."

Sara grinned silently, but Molly was less attuned to such silliness. Molly laughed uncomfortably with a shake of her curly thick hair. "You're a jokester, Amii. Nobody can make it rain."

"Ohhh, I'm serious! A bit of drum beating like a dance here and there."

Molly scowled. "Yea, right, Amii. You're gonna make it rain."

"Why not! I think I'll have to try!" Amii was still playing around yet it humored her a bit that Molly was taking

this seriously. She was just about to do a
little jiggle in a circle and prance a bit
when Sara screamed.

A smooth-skinned frog plopped it's
round green-gray belly next to Sara's
foot. Sara recoiled at the sight of the
amphibian. Jumping back, lifting a leg
hiked high, Sara clamped onto Molly's
arm. Then Sara shuddered whilst
attempting to hide behind Molly. "It's
alright," Molly pulled her partner out
from behind her and giggled while
rubbing Sara's shoulders. "Relax.
Awwww. It's only a frog. Not gonna
bite ya!" Scuffing her foot back and
forth on the dirt before looking up so that
the lollygagging friendly fellow frog
hopped away two feet. "You're not
serious, right? 'Bout makin' it rain?"
(Miraculum was watching these goings-
on with amusement now!)

"Mmm-hmn! Looks like I might as
well."

Molly didn't know quite how to be silly or make a joke, finding Amii's statement to be incorrigible! "You can't!"

"Ohhh. Why not?"

"Because!" She was actually getting angry! Molly was practically frothing! "It's impossible!"

Molly's words caused Ami to think of a song from an old movie she'd once seen; thus softly she began to sing it; yet the words escaped her. "It's impossible, for a horse to be a carriage," she gently serenaded. "No, no, that's not how the song goes." Looking up at a bird in the sky she let go trying to remember the song and simply sighed. "Hmmn." Amii raised her arms up to float in the air around her and walked toe to toe like a tight-rope walker on the boulder. "Life itself is an impossibility Molly."

"Look! I'm a Chemical Engineer! I *know* that there is not…" She stopped short, shook her curly-haired head, actually rivaled with angry indignation and irritation.

Sara yanked on Molly's hand slightly bouncing her knees: "Please don't get started... don't get loud like that... Stop it Molly, I don't want you angry today."

"I'M NOT...!" Molly rolled her eyes, cleared her throat. "I'm not angry, okay?" Molly kissed the tip of Sara's nose to soothe her worries away, then turned to wrinkle her brow at Amii. She lifted her hands in the air as if pleading with Amii. She was really taking this seriously. "Amii, I like you. You're a terrific person. But I'm a chemical laboratory analyst, so believe me, I know what I'm talkin' about when I say ya can't make it rain."

Amii was not good at 'chit-chat' to begin with. Thus she was inclined to simply be *quiet* at such a time as this and let the other person talk all they wanted even if she didn't agree at all, and even if she realistically had a truly better argument. Yet for lack of anything better to talk about the absurdity of Molly's anarchist mitigation rather tickled Amii and appeared reason enough, for at least a trivially small amount of time, to argue for argument's sake! "Molly. I know there is no such thing as supernatural phenomena. All phenomena naturally abide by the laws of physics. Yet there are still some things not yet discovered and understood scientifically, you must admit."

"Amii! Izah' clear, *cloudless*, sky! That…Aaaaah! FINE! Make it rain!"

Amii giggled. "Alright I will! If I make it rain, you owe me a soda; if I don't make it rain I'll buy both you and Sara sodas."

Sara waved her long sandy hair behind one shoulder: "Molly, calm down."

"SARA, I'M CALM!" She rolled her eyes then cleared her throat again. "I mean…will you stop saying that? Please?"

"I'm sorry Molly. I just want us ta' have a good time today."

"We will Sara, I promise." She looked up at their guest Amii playing tight-trope with her feet on the boulder as if she didn't have a care in the world. "We're just standin' here, waitin' for Amii ta' make it rain! So? Prove it!"

"I will prove it, alright? I will prove it, but even if I don't, then either way we'll have sodas!" Amii giggled. She wanted gray sky, she honestly did want a gray wet sky. Yet it truly was a cloudless day. Walking onto the center of the boulder, Amii scanned the desert looking ground. Scattered bits of sweet-grass on the wind-less day. Small bright orange flowers scattered across tiny purple blossoms, a few wide-petal teacup size pink flowers. She felt that on top the huge rock was an appropriate place to scan the arid beauty. Lifting her arms out truly standing tall, Amii held her face to the sky while she giggled again quietly under her breath. Feeling a calm sense of spirit: "Rain," Amii said, "Rain from the heart. Rain from the soul. Rain of the spirit that lives forever." To everyone's surprise the windless day changed so that a slight waft of breezes stirred everyone's hair.

Swirling instantly, then a whooshing gust suddenly hit everyone's body; all were electrically surprised! Amii didn't know what to make of it but she was interested in the sudden winds and chose not to waver. Standing firmly footed on the giant rock, she secretly wished it really *would rain* when a massive blow of winds coincidentally came up from nowhere; it was funny to her. Arms held high, face still to the sky, Amii wondered if anyone was as astounded as she to see that from the completely empty sky white *clouds were now appearing and slowly folding in and out of one another* from the once clear above! Amii wondered if anyone else felt a sense of 'Good', and a sense of Beauty without suffering... a sense of Loving Spirit? This feeling came coincidentally with changes in the sky above them. It was so unusual an unexpected. Billowing, flowing, mixing; growing darker. *What a sight!* What a fabulous wondrous miraculous sight! Deep dark black clouds now began to furl; folding in and out around each other in the sky! Becoming a spreading huge plethora of gray deep-black clouds! Tremendous clouds. Now furling wider. Growing darker. *Rushing in!* The deepest, darkest, blackest clouds began whirling from the center until they became enormous! Sky all around washing gray. Winds higher, harder! Blowing now with great *force*! Grumble like drums from the distance.

Thunder peeled like the sound of rumbles heard from inside the womb. Clouds like painted warriors, from a thousand different tribes, rolling clouds changing shape. Wind flowing, soaring, swooping! Drifting thunder floating in, growing, growing in immensity as a constant pounding rhythm, getting louder. Thunder now a sound like graceful herds of horses running... their hooves pounding on hard solid ground. Horses running rumbles. Shaking growing thunder... pounding closer...louder. Closer!

Slamming synchronized orchestra of deep low-bass drums from a hundred Indian tribes beating out their drumming hides all at once! Low – floating – deep-bass-drum – reverberating round, swooping down, horse hooves running rumbles joining in the echo womb, forming one big span then *BOOM!* Crash of thunder like no other as to quake the very earth; to actually feel it in

the body! Lightening coursed the sky
like fingers, crackling into long-streaked
vibrant flashes. Drops of rain. Drip.
Drop. Drip, drop. Drip, drop. Drip,
drop. Droplets falling larger. Rain
suddenly splashing! Rain streaming like
unstoppable tears all around Amii, Sara,
Molly, in fact the entire desert town!
Rain waters. Sky waters. Strong soul
waters. Salt-less shedding tears. Spirit
rains flowing, blowing, wet-winds
crashing down on Amii's body; she did
not waver. Molly and Sara huddled,
crouching against the wind, drenched in
surprising rain. Standing solid, legs firm,
Amii held her arms wide open;
succumbed to awe.

Dark sky. Drops letting go on Amii's
body, and she would carry it. Love
filling her… breathing love… breathing
deep, over-flowing joy circling through
her hands and feet. Rain; viciously hard
now in pelting streams. Wind crushing
down around a magnanimous thrust.

Crash!—Thunder creaking, groaning,
like the bones of a giant dinosaur
crumbling down to the ground. It's
bones slowly tumbling. One hundred
loud cracking ripples. Shaking crackle in
the air like an old bone-limb breaking.

Screeching rumbling down with the
fingers of lightening streaking all
around—*BOOM*! Bass drum whirling's.
Light flashing. Snapping tapping peals
echoing off into the distance. Sudden
softening of wind from the rolling blow.
Softer still. Wafting, slowing, gentling
gust.

Caressing winds. Kissing winds.
Rain slow. Small wet drop kisses
trickling in the air. Clouds swirling
upward, centering into one another. Blue
sky showing in the dissipating clouds.
Floating clouds wafting in wisps toward
the sun just melting away. Baby-blue
sky surrounding. Sweet air rain-smell.
Clean scented as cave waters. The storm
tempest finished.

Looking from the clear and now once again cloudless sky to the field, flowers were wet-covered as if with dew, yet their petals remained undisturbed. Sun streamed down like soft gold fire.

Filling her nostrils with the air, Amii wet-dripping breathed in deeply. Sugar smell of chlorophyll and earth. Fresh the taste in Amii's mouth; like nutrients mixed with distilled water. Birds flapping their wings lofted into the air. Flying birds on wing towards the sunlight with cheerful twitters; soft singing after the massive rain. Yawning from one end of the horizon to the other was a grand rainbow. Bright, wide, sparkling, rainbow colors. Full light spectrum from red to purple.

Miraculum had prayed for it to rain. Rain for Amii! He prayed, 'Oh Lord, let it rain, a storm the likes of which few have ever seen! Let it rain for Amii!' He had stood up to the side of Amii just below the boulder, legs spread, and his arms wide open. He prayed. Taking his queue from Amii saying she loved rain, he had thought of the unconditional love he felt for his Heaven and his Family, with the emergent desire for Amii to have the thunderstorm she wanted. He let go his love flow and prayed deeply. He never knew if his prayer had helped or not. But *oh*, came the audacious miraculous storm! No-one on this planet will ever know what really happened that day. Was it Amii's wish that had something to do with it despite how nonsensical that sounds? Was it Miraculum's fervent prayer? Could it have been Molly's irritated defiance for an argument? Likely not; not any of that. It was most likely simply one great, big, huge, coincidence! Yet what a coincidence! Not a single person in that town that day will ever forget the event.

*   *   *

The rain stopped and the clouds receded into near instantaneous disappearance. There was now literally not even one single cloud in the sky. Empty blue. Amii turned around with arms still outstretched as she joyously jumped off the boulder, landing down on one knee because she had forgotten about her weak ankles. She hopped back up to stretch the calves of her legs easing the pain in her ankles. She was grinning widely and said, "What a bizarre coincidence! I can't believe that happened!" Molly and Sara were so surprised that it seemed they hadn't even heard what Amii said. All three of them were completely dripping, soaking-wet, drenched!

"I…I…," Molly walked forward mouth-open, and patted Amii on the shoulder, "I'd have never believed it." Pausing, her chin dropped. Molly burst into a smile, slapped her hands together, rubbed a hand over her eyebrows; shook her head from side to side. She bent forward letting out a cheerful laugh before looking up at Amii, whence she said with pure exalted excitement, "Holy shit!" Molly put her hands on either side of her head slowly nodding from left to right. "I don't believe it! You made it rain!" She hopped her shoulders up and down then pointed to the sky. "Look! LOOK! There's not a cloud in the sky! I'd have never believed it if I hadn't seen it with my own two eyes!" Bending over for belting laughter Molly raised her hands in the air thus turning in a circle she looked up. She smiled at Amii. Her arms flung wide open and she took a deep inward breath before wrapping her arms around Amii in a tremendous tremulous wet hug. Amii hugged her back, she liked hugs. "You did it! I can't BELIEVE IT!!" Rocking her now in the hug, "You… you…" Molly let go of her embrace tightly grasping Amii's shoulders; "You made it rain!" She shook her head again. "Well I'll be! I'll be!"

"Molly?" Sara tottered tentatively toward her friend. Tugging a strand of her hair and twirling it: "I wanna go shopping."

Molly paced back and forth several times, talking more as if to herself: "Shopping. Yes, and I'd like ta' get some coffee; I wanna get some coffee, and sit down, and just think about this." Molly halted, spine straight. "Shopping?" Swinging around in one big smiling move putting her arm around Sara: "Yes." Molly began walking forward in long, wide, steps, pulling Sara along. Staring at the ground as if in deep thought: "Yes, yes. Shopping and coffee, yes, alright."

"Or soda's", Amii chuckled.

"Come along Amii;" said Sara with a tupelo honey smile, "Let's go down to the shops and dry off!"

Amii hopped along beside them. All three of them walked down the hill towards the shops. People stood in the muddy wet dirt road completely wet themselves, while others stood outside under the awnings of the shops pointing at Amii whispering amongst themselves in stunned awe that 'That girl had stood on top of the hill and made it rain. They had all seen it. Did you see it?'—They asked each other for nodding affirmations. Miraculum stood watching the three girls chatting and walking down the hill toward the shops. A bright white light began to glow, a light that only Miraculum could see. He was rushed with joy, for as he turned, he knew that now he would be going Home. Miraculum walked toward the light and saw a most magnificent 'presence.'

NINE

A bright white light began to glow tall and wide behind Miraculum. Miraculum turned towards the light that only he could see for he had felt it's presence. He walked towards it with hope in his heart. Perhaps he would go Home now. As he approached the light which seemed to come up from the ground he saw an old man dressed in a robe that made him look like some sort of wizard. The man had kind eyes and a gentle manner and held his hand out to Miraculum. Miraculum took the man's hand and walked into the light with him.

Miraculum found himself in a green luscious meadow full of the most beautiful and colorful array of flowers.

There was a table and two chairs in the soft grass. Yet all around in every direction where there should have been a horizon there was nothing but white light. Above him where there should have been sky there was nothing but white light. White light is the atomic combination of all colors, he thought to himself as he looked around.

"I am Nnema," said the old man with the long whitened hair and long curling aged beard. "Please;" gestured Nnema, "Sit down."

Miraculum circled the chairs and table while Nnema waited patiently for his guest to sit down first. As Miraculum circled round he eyed Nnema suspiciously, and asked, *"Who are you?"*

Nnema folded his hands together in front of his abdomen and said, "I am Nnema. Amii's guide."

"Guide of what?"

"Her life."

"Life?"

"Life, in a human body, while she is on earth. *Please*, do sit down."

Miraculum sat down and so Nnema took a chair as well and sat. Nnema waved his hand above the table as if he were circling a small invisible ball. An ornate bottle of wine encrusted with jewels and thin gold brocade lines appeared where he had waved his hand. Then Nnema again waved his hand yet this time in a smooth semi-circle whereby two bejeweled pewter goblets appeared. Miraculum had been watching him with great interest. Nnema then floated the *back* of his hand in the air in a straight line, and behold a large loaf of steaming fresh bread on a silver platter appeared. Miraculum was impressed and eyed the strange man next to him with increasing wonder. Nnema lifted the bottle of wine in both hands and looked up into Miraculum's eyes as he asked, "Wine?"

"Wine!?" Miraculum couldn't believe it. Could he actually drink it?

Smiling, Nnema filled both goblets full of a deep purple and crimson wine without spilling a drop from the lovely bottle. He set the bottle down and with a gesture of his open arm asked, "Bread?"

Miraculum leaned to look at the deliciously buttery scented loaf. "How do I even know it's bread?"

Nnema gently used the fingers of both his hands and pulled a piece of bread off of the loaf. He dipped the bread in his wine and put it on his tongue, letting it melt in his mouth a moment before he chewed. Next Nnema broke off another piece of bread and dipped it this time into the goblet of Miraculum's wine. He held it with one hand cupped beneath it and leaned towards Miraculum whom also leaned forward. "Bless you my child," said Nnema as he brought the wine-dipped bread to Miraculum's mouth. Parting his red–orange lips Miraculum opened wide, allowing Nnema to place the bread in his mouth; he too let it melt for a moment before he chewed then swallowed.

Leaning over his goblet, Miraculum sniffed at the wine. Then he raised an eyebrow as with a great grin he lifted the goblet and drank down all the wine until he had emptied it. Nnema chuckled and lifting the bottle once again filled Miraculum's goblet full of wine. Miraculum leaned back in his gilt and brocade chair to ask, "So exactly what is it you do?"

"Basically I just follow Amii around." Nnema sipped from his goblet.

"And what does that mean?"

"Well," began Nnema as he swallowed another sip, "it means I am

Amii's observer of her lifetime. It means I am her *witness*."

"Do you ever help her?"

Nnema looked down at his goblet, fingering the jewels laid in the pewter, and with what looked like a bit of sadness in his eyes answered, "Sometimes; when I can."

"Was it hard to figure out?"

"What?"

"That you were to be her *witness*."

"Oh, no, no," chuckled Nnema, "That is something I knew from the beginning. What I can't figure out --- is <u>*you*</u>."

Miraculum had absolutely no idea how to respond to that, so he seized his goblet, drank the entire contents down, then held the goblet in the air with his extended arm and grinning ridiculously as he had seen Amii do when she was on stage, demanded happily, "More wine!"

Nnema chuckled as he refilled Miraculum's elixir of purple-crimson wine. Yet Miraculum merely sat the pewter cup down without even tasting of the sweet-sour liquid. "So what do I do?," asked Miraculum as his expression turned serious.

"I can't tell you precisely what to do." Nnema leaned back to rest his shoulders against the resplendent chair. "Oh I knew Amii would come across evil at some point or other…"

"So you think I'm *evil*!?," roared Miraculum with a pound of his fist upon the table! "I'll have you know when my Home-Planet was made, it was called 'Good'!" Miraculum was incensed. "In *my* Heaven we are One with one another in a way you will never understand! We have joy, eternal happiness, and *unconditional* love!" He pounded his fist again upon speaking the word 'love'.

"Yes, yes, please forgive me if I offend," Nnema rested his elbow upon the table and raised his palm up pleadingly. "Please understand that if I could say 'red' for this, and 'blue' for that, I would. It would still be a description of a light spectrum. Each color one can see is really just a different vibration of light, but we must have words for things. We must describe things with words in order to have understanding of them." Nnema took in a deep breath. "Yet if I said red for good and blue for evil it wouldn't make sense; you understand?"

Miraculum not wishing for Nnema to know that he had absolutely no idea what the old man was talking about, tapped his chin with a finger, nodding his head, and pretended to be in contemplation. "You still haven't told me what I can do," said Miraculum as he placed his arms down upon the chair's armrests.

Nnema placed two fingers over his eyelids then sighed and looked into the meadow about ten feet from the table. Miraculum looked over as well and saw appear two tall rectangular doors made of light with many different colors of the rainbow swirling pretty within them. Miraculum stood up first; then followed by the standing of Nnema, the two of them both walked over to the doors. Miraculum had an expression of awe while Nnema looked worried. "What is this?"—demanded Miraculum.

"They are apparently two paths you can choose from."

"What does it mean?"

To answer Miraculum Nnema would have to feel the energy of each door. Thusly Nnema placed a hand next to the first door. "Ah! This door will take you back to your 'Home'." Nnema next placed his hand against the second door, closed his eyes a moment then savagely shuddered. He looked up at Miraculum with consternation, breathing inward deeply before saying, "By the pull of this second door, I would say it is a human lifetime."

"Human!?"

"Yes."

"I can do that?"

"Yes."

Miraculum was flabbergasted! He placed his hand against the first door of light to feel in his surprise the depthless heart-wrenching longing to go Home. Turning his face away from Nnema's gaze, he nearly choked in the surge of stinging tears that welled up in his eyes. Yanking his hand away he forced a cough and wiped his face with a long rough pull of his palm to smear aside the evidence of his solemn wet ribbons of lamentation. Miraculum paced. His mind whirling. Turning in temerarious flagrance he gave Nnema a glare of telltale trembling vexed infliction. He tensed his arm muscles in taut raised fists, enchanted his eyes towards the absent heavens, roaring: "I have more faith than anyone! I am *not* a monster! I have the greatest faith of *all*!" Slanting his eyes sideways he was taken aback by Nnema's wincing expression.

"So sorry," sputtered Nnema realizing his indignant indiscretion. "I can never quite get used to the way your kind *roar.*"

This statement surprised Miraculum entirely; for if he had been back Home his entire family would have felt his exuberance also and roared right along with him!

Stepping forward with a heart full of stabbing compassion that lurched and convulsed upward into his throat, Nnema spoke with soothing kindness, melting gentleness: "Take my advice; *go Home.*"

"I want to *know*!"—roared Miraculum! "I want the knowledge of the universe, and beyond! *I... want... to...understand*!" Quivering tremors of breath trespassed from his lungs in treacherous windy expulsions as he fought back an assault of more burning wet ribbons that threatened their way into his watering eyes. "I have the greatest faith of them all!"

Sensing he should step backward away from the doors a couple of feet to maintain the aplomb self-possession of his safety, Nnema did just that. Opening his hands in a gesture of protective reassurance, Nnema said to Miraculum: "Whatever you choose Miraculum, may love and blessings follow you always. You *will* have Peace when you are done."

Miraculum marched stolidly back over to the table, turning around to face the doors with telestic temerity; holding wake with certain demonstrable resolve.

Placing one hand on the table he posed as
if a runner about to shoot off in a
marathon. Emboldened stern intention
hardened his face; Miraculum began
screaming. Screaming as if to hone in on
the kill. Miraculum rocked procumbent
de novo on his feet, then in full powerful
force sprinted into a thudding pounding
run, screaming all the while! He leapt
through... *the second door*!

"Peace be with you child," whispered
Nnema softly as he shook his head from
side to side and watched both doors
disappear.

Miraculum found himself falling,
falling, and falling; screaming
continuously in his downward declivity.

TEN

Miraculum entered a foggy hazy phase which he thought a dream. He saw it as if from up above: Amii, in a town of a U.S. place he knew intuitively was called California. It was from another comedian theater, he somehow knew, that she had gone with three of the other comics to the store. Unfortunately, as he watched aghast, that one of the performers said to her: "I have to stop off at this warehouse. It will only take a little while." Miraculum watched from above as if his spirit were in the rafters while the three male performers sat on wood crates at a barrel in the middle, and played cards while drinking beer in the warehouse. Amii grew tired of waiting for the performers to finish whatever business they had intended here in the ugly stark warehouse. Miraculum intuited that Amii thought they were waiting for a friend of theirs; so she politely waited also. Eventually as the hour waned onward Amii told the three men she would go outside and get some air…and 'would they be much longer'— she had inquired. The men said, 'not much longer', thus Amii went outside the warehouse only to be wholly surprised that it was dark outside, since they had left to go to the store when it was still daylight. Miraculum watched more as if he were floating in the sky above Amii, as the three men exited the warehouse, jumped into the Cadillac vehicle, and *despite Amii running along behind the car waving her arms and shouting*, the men took off in a rushed wheel-squeaking screech, leaving her behind them, alone! Miraculum thought he was dreaming; he felt as if he were now just a few feet above Amii's head while he watched her walk to a grocery store and

buy sleeping pills and a box of razor
blades. Still at this smoky-misty phase
he watched without feeling anything at
all; no emotion; nothing. Following
along just a few feet above her head,
Miraculum took in the scene as Amii
crossed a street to a convenience store.
In the store, Amii asked what town she
was in. Miraculum felt shocked, dream
or not, that she had been abandoned in a
town she didn't even know the name of!
Tall and handsome whilst very well
dressed, a man was listening to Amii
speak with the store clerk while he
picked up an iced coffee for himself; he
seemed keen with interest. The clerk
told Amii what town she was in, which
clearly rang zero bells for the girl. Also,
the clerk informed Amii where a hotel
was, but it was several miles away. It
was at this time the handsome gentleman
bought his iced coffee and offered Amii a
ride to the afore mentioned hotel. Amii
accepted, since Miraculum sensed, Amii
knew she could not walk so far with her

weak ankles. The well-dressed man had a savvy red sports car, and Miraculum watched as he dropped Amii off at the specified hotel. In his 'dream' Miraculum toyed with the small plastic bag Amii had from the grocery store and it's contents accidentally spilled out. Next in his dream Amii gushed in a lungful of air embarrassment whilst she put the boxes of sleeping pills and razor blades back into the bag. There was a moment where Miraculum felt in this dream as if he were sitting near between Amii and this man whom had offered the ride; Miraculum watched with interest as the man looked frightened and tried to get Amii to take some of his money with her in case she needed it. Yet Amii refused the money saying she did not need it, left the red sports car which took off and away; she then bought a room with the last bit of cash she had…oddly enough, she had just barely enough for the room. Miraculum continued to watch this dream. In it he saw Amii draw a cool bath inside her hotel room; watched her fill the sink with warm water. She took off all her clothes which meant a blurry nothing to him; and then he watched her as she looked into the mirror at the sink. Amii poured a glass of water from the sink tap, and counted out six sleeping pills. She swallowed the pills and watched the clock for twenty minutes… he guessed that in the dream she was waiting for the pills to make her sleepy. At last twenty minutes lapsed and she pulled her left arm back flat; a razor in her right hand. In the dream Miraculum saw Amii place her left wrist into the sink water, whereby she cut medically precisely and quite directly along the major wrist's vein approximately an inch and a half. Since it was precisely upon the vein, blood whirled flooding gushes in watery pulsing circles into the water-filled sink. He sensed in the dream that the cut was far more painful than the girl had expected! She then walked fast to the tub and lay down in it…. It seemed she did not wish to make a big mess for the hotel to have to clean up after her. A fully opened vein beneath the water roared out forcefully quick to turn the bath-tub water into a pure deep ruby blush. Miraculum watched the dream with fascination until Nnema appeared! Then, appeared many angels in various forms, and even in shapes of vibrating colorful rainbow-filled light! Surpassing surprise adrenaline-terror shook Miraculum as Nnema's face rushed up towards his own face! Nnema slapped Miraculum so hard it sent a sobering stall of consciousness to stand still at attention immediately! Nnema spoke not a single word as Miraculum realized…this is not a dream! *Passing it might be, but for the moment not a dream*!

Miraculum looked at the angels all about and at last heard them saying she can not die for she must do.. then the words were lost. Nnema's slap had stalled him from his slumberous numbness. Post haste Miraculum followed a string of energy which took him to his desired destination of the man in the red sports car whom already had a car phone in his hands. Miraculum shouted with all his soul to the man: "Call emergency for the girl" This man heard the voice of Miraculum which shook him frightened for a second; then he fraught the experience off and dialed the U.S. telephone number for emergency; he told the operator where the girl was precisely, what he had seen in her plastic grocery bag, and that they had better hurry for he felt she meant to commit suicide! At peace with the man's actions Miraculum flew back to the hotel room to find it empty of any spirits! He coaxed her with his yearning alone to get out of the tub and wrap her wrist in a towel. She did just that to his relief; then she lay down on the bed and pulled the covers over herself. A knocking at the door proved to be the police and paramedics. She told them through the closed door there must be some mistake; that she was fine; for them to go on away. (They busted in the door.) Then as they looked at her in the covers they chuckled when she said she had taken six sleeping pills that seemed not to be working, and they felt the whole scene was nothing but tomfoolery. Until Miraculum tugged at one policeman's sleeve to look at the sink! Indeed the policeman looked at the blood filled watery sink, then at the blood all over the sink's counter. The policeman followed the blood all over the carpet, then halted when he saw the blood-filled bathtub! "Come here!"—the policeman said to his comrades; and they all looked at the ruby water...the thick blood trail which led to the bed. She must be bleeding profusely! They begged her to remove the bed covers, and she refused as she was naked. Yet it was then that Miraculum had another most profound epiphany! 'Evil must not be allowed to harm Good...

Good must be protected… and who
better than He to do such a job?' Thus
Miraculum leapt into the body of a police
officer with dark brown crisply cut hair
on his head, and zero hair on his face.
Inside the police officer's body he
coaxed Amii to show them the small but
straight on the vein chugging cut.
Miraculum in the man's body held
Amii's hand in the ambulance; and said,
"Well you certainly got my attention."
His face was furrowed in love and worry
and he held her hand at the hospital while
they sewed back the vein then sewed the
muscle and at last sewed the skin…it was
all very nice tight stitches. Then
Miraculum felt a force, an energy;
perhaps an actual individual, pulling him
away from Amii as she lay looking into
his eyes in the hospital bed. The 'dream'
was fading away. "NO!"—Miraculum
screamed against being pulled away from
Amii!! "*NO*!!"

Miraculum kept screaming, yet it was with a fierce burning determination. As he fell through a swirling tunnel of white light which sparkled here and there in pastels of blue, pink, and green, he thought to himself that if he were (abhor the thought) evil, then fine! He would think of his evilness as a divine talent and use that 'talent' for 'good' conclusion. He held on to this thought with massive strict intention through wavering bouts of faintness that dizzyingly wrought at his consciousness like a vapid lethal anesthetic capable of rendering him lost into the void. Gluing the thought to his soul so that it was like a flower, a fully blossomed sweet ruby blushed rose, that for an hallucinated moment he actually saw and smelled floating spiral down into his cupped hands. Finally he waned into the liquid darkness of unconsciousness to come out the other side of the lighted tunnel *a screaming little scrawny crack-addicted baby boy, with two red circular birthmarks on his head directly where his horns had been*!

His parents named him Michael, after the archangel that slays demons; (heaven help the boy.). Also, had his parents known that by telling the truth and saying to the nurses and physicians that they would in fact go right back to using methamphetamine as soon as they left the hospital; which was most sadly certainly the truth, they would not have been allowed to keep the baby boy, then they would have copped to it and immediately said so right away! Yet out of the fear of being arrested, Michael's parents denied it indubitably, saying that now they were 'clean' they were going to stay clean. Thus the hospital dispatched Michael into his parents care whereby both parents, baby in tote, went home straight away to begin smoking methamphetamine once more.

If it weren't for the use of day-care Michael might have died from starvation from the very beginning! Yet, thanks to low cost day care, Michael received government funded formula; later baby-food, then as time passed he grew into such yummies as cheese, milk, sandwiches, and cookies. His hair flossed thickly when he'd still been just a little baby, growing quite dark and frothy over his birthmarks. Michael grew to cherish the three and four day spans when his parents would at last fall into a deep sleeping stupor after having been awake without a nod of sleep for an entire week! They'd start off happy and jumping then wind down cranky before leaving him to some peace as they fell into long bouts of dreamless oblivion. The young boy would not have known the difference had someone told him it was merely a peculiar natural occurrence of his parent's circadian rhythm to stay awake nocturnally as by sunlight for days on end then sleep long periods of time in a seemingly shameless comatose-shaded stunpoll! Of course it was indeed a most un-natural onus onslaught caused by the bathtub chemistry they soaked up in wild-eyed puffs. Oh my, but this did not bother Michael in the least for when his bony parents fell out into their ensanguined enslaved slumber he could watch television to his hearts bouquet. Young son Michael did not like the children's television shows, which somehow he took most personally to be quite silly, heaven knows why, so he immersed himself in what he craved…a knowledge of a greater sort. Thus he watched with reverence many documentaries; reveled in lovely bits about history and science! He learned that no government anywhere had the right to take away those plants which grow naturally to the earth from those humans which are also natural to the earth. That prohibition of alcohol had begun the mafia in America. That prohibition of natural plants had begot gangs. This begot the grotesque creations of bathtub chemistry which is sorely unnatural, and thus caused gut-rot in prohibition days, and unbeknownst to him his parents fell into the next category, came bathtub chemistry attempting to supposedly imitate natural plants but being unnatural to a fact merely rotted the body including the brain. Documentaries informed him clearly of the science of that which is natural to the earth and all it's living creatures, including marvelous cures coming directly from the rainforest; of fabulous flowers, leaves, and mushrooms! However, it sat as an intrepid intuition to Michael the fair certainty that perhaps his parents were un-naturally rotting themselves (despite his childhood yearning to hope the best of his mother and father.) His hilarity and muffled guffaws circled his spirit once in a documentary he'd seen on television one sunny, blue-sky afternoon while his parents lay inert, where all these animals, to Michaels fanciful surprise, zebras, giraffe, monkeys, antelope, elephants, and even huge regal lions, gathered at this place…. Not a one of them eating or even slightly tormenting the other, as they placidly waited for these tree berries to naturally ferment, until the fattened over-ripe berries plopped heavy to the ground in great piles. Michael giggled, chuckled, held his ribs, as he watched all the animals, predators and vegetarians alike, eat the berries until they were tipsy-topsy drunk. Also, the young boy soaked in like a warm ray of sunshine scientists discussing the planets, and physics; historians reminiscing. Oh, the marvel of Edgar Allen Poe; or even of the profound keen warrior expertise of the terrible barbarous Genghis Khan! Michael was a little human boy enamored with learning!

Miraculum, now the child 'Michael', knew he had a talent, although he could not yet fathom what it was, he knew he had one. Spending odd days sitting upon the window sill gleaming respectfully at the birds nesting in the corner of the covered patio outside, he'd rub his chin, nod his head, moan and hum in contemplation, searching for that special talent. He would often run up to his parents with one of his 'talent ideas' to say out loud full of innocence and excitement, "I know what I want to be when I grow up! I want to be a surgeon! Then I could get into all that bloody, brainy, gunk and pull out the bad stuff, and it will be great, great fun, and I will have helped someone!"

Now any other parent would have looked down, smiled at their child's glowing face, patted them on the head at the gleeful exclamation, saying: 'Good job son. You do that!' *Not Michael's parents*. They had a completely different response to any of their boy's grand ideas on what he wanted to be when he grew up. Michael's mother would scream, "You stupid know-it-all! You think you're so smart! You're nothing!

You're *nothing*!" Then she would back-hand Michael so hard across the face that it would knock him off his feet! This would follow with his father coming at him shrieking, "Now look what you've made your mother do!"—kicking his son blasphemously bitter-hard so that the boy would literally tumble clear across the room! Brain-soaked bathtub poisonous chemistry in bowline adrenocortical rage flew the boy's father into kicking him, kicking him; his mother joining in the mad beating, until Michael usually ended up a bloody pulp.

Next his parents would stuff him into the small space beneath the shelves in the kitchen pantry. They'd put a swatch of carpet on the small pantry floor to help soak up the blood, feces, or urine, since cleaning it was such a bother. Shutting the pantry door, leaving him there as if it were an oubliette. Ah, but this did not last long! When they figured out that after coming to consciousness and waiting a while Michael would push open the door and get out, the man and woman were nonplussed with annoyance. It was then his parents decided to spend some of their not-so-well-earned money to buy a door with a lock on the *outside*. Meticulously they installed the door in the small third bedroom, on the doorframe of the terribly tiny closet, which to their relief already had carpet in it --good for soaking up unwanted human secretions of stinking messy sticky liquids.

Beating Michael up upon their inexplicably foul rages seemed to them good proper character-building punishment for what they considered incorrigible impudence. They decided it was simply 'training their child'. Putting him in the teeny closet, closing the door, locking it from the outside so that he could not get out, gave them a sense of peace whereby they both would most often forget about him for days.

Sometimes they would even go looking for him before they recalled they had him still locked in the closet. One such torrentially unfortunate time the couple had crammed Michael into the stifling humid oppressively-airless closet with his body broken, black-rose bruised, bleeding nasty red-rose streams, locked the door from the outside, then proceeded to forget about him for an entire week!

Somehow upon the seventh day of Michael's forgotten capture locked in the closet, his parents were in a particularly jolly mood, deciding they would buy pizza and share it with their son. The couple searched all about the house for their boy before they remembered he was still in the closet. Opening the closet door announcing that he had been well, duly, properly punished and could come out now, they were thrust into a panic. His ashen crumpled body looked to the parents as if he were... well... not right. Upon closer inspection with his arms

over his head as if trying still to protect
himself from swollen blows, they
realized to a high-piercing pulverizingly
pungent pandemonium that their son was
not privy to life anymore; Michael was
dead! Prying the colorless prosaic of
Michael's body out of the small space
they warranted the preposterous pretext
that it was all Michael's fault that things
had come to this lethal end. Discharging
a quilt to wrap him in, they both
frantically paced in wild prickly
disturbing confusion. Haste was
precisely the prescription for this
perplexing dilemma, if only the man and
woman of yellowing rotten skin and
bones might pull in the reins to their
stampede of hysteria! Panicked, pacing,
yelling at one another, saying they had to
think, think think! Until at last it was
decided in sweaty frantic agreement that
they would simply have to bury
Michael's body.

Waiting to the stroke of midnight, despite the moon being too bright for their taste, the couple took a shovel and spade in hand, along with a piece of baby-blue pipe; they dug a hole in the back yard. Tumbling Michael's placid body into the hole, covering the child with dirt, they set about masking the grotesqueness in this deed by picking grass and leaves to cover over the spot. Sweaty dirt clung to them both in the rasp finalization as they stuck the blue pipe to a standing position in the fresh turned dirt to mark the grave; because being superstitious, they did not want to accidentally forget where the grave was, step on it, and get bad luck.

Michael (truly Miraculum), watched the entire event from 'out of his body'. He had watched his parents open the closet door to discover his dead body as he stood behind them the whole time! He had watched them dig the grave; seen his parents slump his battered broken body of blood and bruises into the crude dirt hole. Yes; oh yes, Michael had watched them jam the baby-blue pole in the balmy dirt muttering about their foolish superstitions!

My, my, but Michael knew now what anger was, oh yes indeed he did! He felt it with abundance! Truly Michael felt himself most unfortunate for surely he had received the worst parents on the planet. He was right! They were a horrid pair. Though they could not see Michael, his parents could feel it when he would push them. When they were outside in the backyard Michael panged every inch of his energy to push and push on either one of them until his mother or father fell onto the gravesite; where they would scramble to their feet flooded

with terror. When Michael was
alive, his parents would smoke
their methamphetamine then go
out into the front yard where
they would drink glass bottles
of beer or sodas or in fact, any
sugary liquid they could get
their hand on; sometimes
adding half cups of granule
sugar to whatever they were
drinking. They just wanted
sugar! For the replenishment
of true nourishment was not as
important to them as the sugar
rush. Emptying their bottles of
it's sugary contents into their
starved acidic stomachs, then
breaking the glass of the bottles
onto the ground where it would
smash into tiny shards, jagged
pieces. Most often they would
break the glass onto the ground
of the front yard directly on top
of where Michael had set his
toys. An act which seemed to

Michael (quite correctly) to be on purpose. Sugar stoned with bathtub chemistry coursing through their veins, soaking and shrinking their brains, his parents would smash the glass bottles on top of where he had set up his little dark green plastic soldier toys. Or where he had lain out his small cars. In the spot his petite irenic plastic house with the roof molded to look like wood logs, the thumb-sized toy family he pretended lived there, suffered the last slum slurp from a glass bottle to wit his mother or father would smite by a crash of glassy smithereens. Michael spent excruciating hours of carefully trying to pick out his soldiers or other toys from the glass without being cut. Ah, things had changed! Now that Michael was dead but still

watching them, his parents
standing out in the front yard
drinking down their syrupy
liquid candy sodas, Michael
unseen would sojourn to smack
the smirk off their faces which
he felt was his suffrage.
Bottles flew out of his parent's
hands in such force invisible
that their sodas would pound
onto the ground in a hale of
broken glass, the sugary
contents seeping like fingers
across the hardened earth
toward exhilarated ants! Paltry
pale festering faces flooded
with fear while gazing
dumbfounded at their broken
sodas, for they could actually
feel the bottle being hit out of
their hands!

One evening in Michael's
ecclesiastical loaming deathful
slumber as his mother was

putting food upon the kitchen
table where his father
anxiously waited, Michael's
ghost knocked a dish smack-
dab out of his mother's hands
whence she approached the
table! The dish smashed and
broke. "THAT'S IT!"--
announced Michael's father as
he slammed his hands against
his knees, "Either you did that
on purpose, or we're out of
here!" ('We're out of here.'—
responded his mother with a
shaking head, knowing her
partner believed her after all
the phantasmic mishaps.)
Michael watched as his parents
rapidly grasped in terror what
they could throw into a couple
of large plastic sacks meant
originally for garbage, not as
luggage, jumping afterwards
hackles raised into their tiny
pick-up truck. In the driveway,

with a loud slamming of two
trucks doors, they drove away,
leaving practically everything
they owned behind.

   The front door stayed unlocked, even
food warm and ready to be eaten still sat
upon the kitchen table. Clothes hung in
the master bedroom closet; furniture
remained to eventually gather dust. The
couple drove far, far away; never to
return. Within a few weeks after the rent
was due, the land-lord came to the house
knocking. No-one answered, so land-
lord let himself in through the unlocked
front door. A stench most putrid wafted
in lazy heated waves so horribly
throughout the house that the fat land-
lord loosened his tie, then running to the
sink full of molding dishes dry-heaved
until his stomach rattled back down.
Items lay scattered about; drawers still
full of clothes. Yet most disgusting to
the land-lord was the molded petrified
food on the table; the un-flushed toilet

full of the germinating contents of someone's intestines. Flies buzzing everywhere, he knew his tenants would not be back. They had skipped out on him! Property is equity, thus the artery-clogged land-lord had the house cleared out and cleaned. Poor workers whom cleaned the carpets, had scrubbed and scoured for meager wages at the little swatch of carpet on the pantry floor; scrupulously cleansing the carpet on the floor of the tiny closet in the small third bedroom. Finally it was with head-hung announcement to the land-lord, they could NOT get those stains out! The land-lord being somewhat stingy refused to change the carpets, not even in the pantry or the third bedroom closet, saying to himself 'clean enough'. That was the end of the matter, let it be a new owner's concern! Three years in a row the land-lord rented to three different families whom each inexplicably left most of their Items behind in a hurried elopement from the house without even

bothering to tell him of their leave!
Saying nothing of their going; staving
address-unknown never to return.
Laying empty for five years after the last
tenant, dear Michael's ghost felt
forlornly lonesome. Occasionally a
family would come and stand out in the
street, looking at the house feeling
inexplicable trepidation, without stepping
one foot near it's yard. They would all
claim a peculiar feeling regarding the
house; no-one would rent or buy. Much
to the land-lords chagrin.

Michael trapped! Once he had tried
to run out into the street to flag down a
passing car, smashed against what was
invisible but felt like glass just at the
edge of the yard. He followed this
surprising smooth barrier only to
discover it barred all around the yard,
both front and back. Also as he slid
across in curiosities horrors, he found it
over the house like a dome. Michael the
forgotten pacing ghost-child unwanted;

Michael the caged lion. Soul-scarring, such pain and loneliness. Trapped!
***Stuck, yes, yet despite the years of zero occupants and no lawn care; except an occasional mowing, the grass was green, the roses and cannas grew lush with flowers. Michael made the best of where he was, taking it upon himself to tend the garden. He loved the roses and cannas flowers whole-heartedly, giving them waves of love straight from his soul making all blossom plumage masterfully beautiful. Concentrating his love of their beauty, transcendent waves of his labor engorged each flower to grow magnificently. Scents of rich petals made a strong sweet wafting perfume. Michael also loved birds, often he sang to a bird when he saw it, sending waves of love to the feathered creatures blessed with wings. Much to his delight, they would nest year after year in the trees of his backyard. Michael laid in the grass many hours with his arms folded beneath his head, looking up into the shimmering

trees during the days of sunlight, the nights of moonlight, admiring the chirping preening birds. Then one day something shocking happened! Michael lazily sat on top of the roof when a family came to look at the house. Yet this time was different, for the man, woman, and their six year old son, did not wrinkle their noses in a stinking feeling of peculiarity then leave. Instead the family marched smiling right up to the house looking pleased to see the brilliant roses and gleaming tall orange cannas. Sniffing the flowers, magnanimous perfume, commenting on it, they walked right through the door and into the house!

Scared, Michael zipped down through the roof to hide in the attic. While hidden with his back against the attic wall he listened to the family's muffled voices, pondering his situation. Over the years Michael had remembered he was really Miraculum, and not 'Michael' at all, yet had a difficult time making sense of it. He remembered just about everything. Remembered who he really was, yet his ties to his lifetime as Michael were so overwhelming he could not change his appearance to his true and preferred form. No matter how hard he concentrated he stayed in the body-form of the six year old Michael; *his mind still that of a child's.* The land-lord wiped his sweaty brow with a yellowed hanky while trailing behind yet staying quiet as the family looked quickly around the house and in the back yard. Much to Miraculum's relief, the family merely peered into the garage, not going into the attic where he trembling lay hid. This house being for sale at a remarkably low price, was a primary reason the female of the family said to the land-lords devout joy, after weaning their way once more to the front yard all smiling thrill, "I'll take it!"

ELEVEN

Miraculum stayed
frightened and hidden in the attic, even
as he listened to the noises of the family
moving in. They had bought the house
he realized leaving him at a loss for what
to do. He stayed in the attic a long time
feeling catastrophically frigid with worry
until one night he heard the family
coming in the front door and he bolstered
up his courage. Dropping down through
the ceiling into a crouching position in
the living room, Michael held his head
down. Still in the physically appearing
body of the six year old child, Miraculum
(Michael) slowly lifted his head, next
raising his eyes, looking firmly at these
intruders! Miraculum watched the

woman kiss both cheeks of the man and say, "Goodnight, we'll see you tomorrow."

"Come here little man," exclaimed the father, who leaned down giving his son a big loving hug. Miraculum looked up from the man and son to the woman; he was astonished! "Ammmii"--Miraculum whispered whilst the woman jiggled a finger in her ear as if she might have heard him. Amii! It was Amii! It was HIS Ami! Miraculum felt thrilled and perplexed at the same time! She was fully grown now, but still so young and beautiful! Looking down at the boy Miraculum deduced the child couldn't be much more than his own age of six years old. The same age he had been when he had died. Looking for rings on the parent's left hands, seeing there were none, he surmised from what he'd seen on television that the two adults were not married. (Truth being, the pair had divorced due to different temperaments,

although doing so amicably. Both still
friends, the father was more than happy
to help them out and come visit his son.)
Miraculum followed Amii and her son
Elijah all around the house day after
unending day with keen interest. He was
pleased to watch Elijah and Amii enjoy
the lightening bugs in the back yard at
night. Little Elijah capturing some of the
small glowing bugs in a jar, poking holes
in the top of it's metal lid.

One seemingly fine day a most bizarre
occurrence took place! Elijah had his
little friend Roy over to play. Amii, a
delightful gentle mother, had made the
two young boys sandwiches. The
youngsters sat in the hallway, their
sandwiches in hand. Roy ate his much
quicker than Elijah. Roy said "I sure am
still hungry!"

"Well here", Elijah offered the other
half of his chewed upon sandwich,
"You're my guest, I want you to have the
rest of my sandwich."

"No"; spoke Roy shuffling his stubby little fingers, "it's yours."

"No," emphatically insisted Elijah, "I want you to have it, really."

"No." Roy shook his head.

"Here," obliged Elijah hopefully, holding the sandwich out toward his friend. "Eat it, I want you to have it."

All at once Miraculum felt an infantile rage of disgust as he watched Roy shake his head 'No' once more to the kindly offered sandwich! Miraculum found it profoundly rude for Roy not to take the sandwich when it had been offered in such genuine politeness. Indignant anger soared through Miraculum so that in deepest rage he drove himself right into the body of Elijah! Eyes glaring shiny, 'Elijah' terrified poor Roy growling in a possessed low-bark toned voice: *"EAT THE SANDWICH!"* Pounding his head down onto Roy's forearm in a fast, bloody, powerful sinking bite of his teeth! Suddenly both Elijah and Miraculum were shocked! Miraculum popped back out Elijah's body feeling shaken… he had just wanted to *help* Elijah! (It would have been fabulously comic. Except alas for the deep bite, the sheer shock.)

"Waa!"--cried Roy, grasping his arm, tears bursting out of his little eyes, as his face turned red.

Alarmed, Amii came running from the kitchen into the hallway. Elijah had his palms turned upwards from his bent elbows with a confused, worried look. (Poor, dear Elijah.) Bewilderment crossed Elijah's face while he stuttered with profundity: "I …I… don't know what happened, Mom! Roy was still hungry, so I offered him my sandwich, then it was like I *fainted* or something! Next thing I knew, I opened my eyes and my face was pressed against his arm!"

"Oh no", soothed Amii to the crying little boy Roy, "Oh dear honey…." She comforted, consoled, as she bent down. "Come here sweetie, let me see." Amii hugged Roy with one arm while placing her fingers on the arm Roy was holding. Looking down, Amii was horrified. Deep teeth-marks set bleeding in Roy's arm. The bite was already bruising black and blue. "You bit him?!" Amii proclaimed this with astonishment.

"I don't know!" Elijah replied helplessly.

"What do you mean you don't know, Elijah? You bit him?"

"I don't know!" Poor child.

Amii lifted Roy up into her arms, cradling, rocking him back and forth. "Elijah! To your room *now*! You're grounded for…" In the chaos she had to actually think of her child's age. "….Six minutes!" One was supposed to only ground a young child one minute per each year of their age. Amii stood up hefting Roy upon her hip while softly pushing Elijah's shoulder with her other hand towards his room. Elijah walked dejected into his room and turned around to say, "*But Mom!*" Amii gently shut Elijah's bedroom door. Miraculum didn't know what to think; he didn't even know he could still enter anyone's body anymore. Miraculum felt awfully sorry for the completely confused Elijah, as he watched Amii put anti-bacterial ointment that contained pain-reliever on Roy's bitten arm. She covered the bite with rainbow colored band-aids, kissed the top of the band-aids with little smooches saying, "All better now, all better." Amii hoisted Roy back onto her hip grateful the pain-reliever in the ointment was working quickly (he wasn't crying anymore.) Roy was happy for the kisses and to simply feel much better. Roy and Miraculum watched as Amii carried the child clinging on her hip back to Elijah's bedroom. Amii walked into Elijah's room to find her son sitting on his bed reading one of his children's books with a most glum expression equipoise his sad face. "Alright now," uttered Amii to Elijah, "You're no longer grounded, but you may never bite anyone ever again. Do you understand this?"

Elijah looked up into his mother's eyes saying sick-hearted, "Yes Mom. I'm Sorry."

"Well, you need to tell Roy you're sorry."

"I'm sorry Roy"

Roy was on to better thoughts now that his arm no longer hurt. He glibbed rather joyfully: "It's okay. Read a book!"

Thinking this a fantastic idea to change the situations mood, Amii chose a couple of Elijah's children's books; picking them up with her free hand (child still set on hip) beckoning Elijah to follow. Amii shuffled into the living room and smiling sweetly for the children so they might feel love sat down, thusly Elijah, Roy, and Miraculum also, sat close to her on the couch, listening while she animatedly read books. The doorbell rang before Amii had finished all the books she'd chosen. It was Roy's mother come to pick him up. Amii raised Roy into her arms, resting him against her hip again to open the door. The child's mother took her son in her arms saying, "Thank you for letting them play."

"Oh, it's my pleasure. I'm glad for Elijah and Roy to be friends. Umm…" Amii pointed at the band-aids, "It would seem Roy and Elijah had a bit of a tiff."

Roy's mother peeled back an edge of the band-aids and gasped at the partial site of the terrible blue-purple bite. "I don't think…Think…"--stammered Roy's mother, "That Roy will be playing with Elijah anymore."

"Oh… Of course," Amii spoke nervously, "I fully understand." What else was there to say? Roy's mother scurried off towards her car, son in her arms, as Amii sorrowfully closed the front door.

*   *   *

Miraculum hid in the attic for quite some time after that unwarranted dishevelment over a measly sandwich; sloshing in confusion, frustration. At last his feelings overwhelmed, kittling into agonizing anger. He held his legs wrapped in his arms, rocking back and forth crying out loud: "I want to die! I want to die! I want to die! I want to go home! I WANT TO GO HOME!" Miraculum's pained soul could stand it no longer, caustically leaping to his feet he shouted out: "Enough is enough!" Miraculum jumped down through the attic floor, landing in a crouch with his head down, still in his form of the six year old Michael. Rolling his eyes, looking up ever so slowly, Miraculum saw he was in the kitchen. Amii was in the living room flipping through video's to find a movie family-friendly enough to watch. Elijah's father stood behind her observing. Elijah was walking into the kitchen; had he been tall enough, he would have grabbed a cup, but since he was still too short to reach the cupboard above the kitchen counter, he figured he would just sneak a drink of milk straight from the jug in the refrigerator. Yet succumbing Elijah had hardly passed the corner of the kitchen counter where the phone sat when Miraculum ran and jumped directly into Elijah's body! Miraculum in Elijah's body, rolled onto the floor, eyes lolling momentarily, then scooted backwards until his spine was against the wall next to the backdoor. He pulled his legs up, wrapped his arms around his knees; began rocking back and forth, back and forth, saying in a dark monotone: "I want to die! I want to die!" Saying it over and over in ghastly non-stop repetition. Amii and her ex-husband jerked towards the open kitchen in horrified response. Amii leapt to her feet, dropping videos, running immediately to her beloved. Elijah's father following close behind. Elijah kept up the rocking back and forth with an un-seeing glaze in his eyes, pallor bloodless skin tightened, droning continuously: "I want to die, I want to die!" Despite all of Amii's gentle, worried pleading and questions he kept it up. Despite his fathers asking "Elijah? Elijah what is wrong?" He kept it on for nearly an *hour*!

Desperation seized Elijah's mother's bones, prickling her inner screaming fears, so she picked up the phone and dialed 9-1-1.

"9-1-1 what's your emergency?"

"My son keeps rocking back and forth and saying he wants to die! And it's been nearly an hour now! Listen to this!" Tremulously Amii held the phone in front of her son's face as he rocked to and fro ingeminating frazzling fire: "I want to die!" Shaking terrified Amii pulled the phone back to her own ear and said in panic, "Did you hear that?!"

"Yes Ma'am," said the female emergency operator. "You must get your son to a hospital, I'll look up the right hospital for your area and call you back."

"Okay!"-- hollered Amii abundantly subjugated in repudiated terror. Then almost as an afterthought: "Thank you!" Slamming down the phone, "Ack!" she shrieked. Amii, shaking her hands and looking with solemn entreaty to Elijah's father, "I didn't give them my address or phone number!"

"Don't worry" tried her ex-husband attempting not to sound as frightened as he felt, " It's 9-1-1 They know where your calling from."

Amii ran to Elijah's bedroom, gathered up his pajama's, his teddy bear; was in the process of running back into the living room to look for a bag to put them in when the phone rang. Shoving the items into her ex-husbands arms, running to the telephone, picking up the receiver breathless! "Hello?"--Amii shouted into the phone. "Yes! Yes!" Amii fumbled for pen and paper near the telephone, writing down the name and address of the hospital the 9-1-1 operator gave her. The emergency operator said she would call the hospital and inform them they were coming. Amii slammed down the receiver again, yet just when she did Elijah stopped saying anything! He crawled, eyes glazed, toward the bathroom. Both parent's sudden stunned silence was apropos for the be-quietude that fell hush upon the home. The fact that Miraculum could tell that Elijah's body needed to urinate was bizarre in his experience; not wishing to embarrass the pitifully strapped Elijah by making him soil himself, he crawled like a wounded animal to the bathroom, lifted the toilet-seat, sat down on the toilet and urinated.

Miraculum lifted up, pulled the boy's pants back up and while still staring glaring fixedly forward reached behind him knocked the toilet-lid back closed and flushed the toilet! The parents of Elijah were peeking into the bathroom with piercing perplexity, Amii asking "Elijah? Are you alright?" Miraculum flung himself onto the floor, began growling. half crawling, half rolling, he pulled himself out of the bathroom and into the hallway, with Amii and her ex-husband backing up. Elijah rolled onto his back with his limbs flailing. He kept on growling. Powerful moonlight glare in his eyes like a struggling animal under a terroristic petrified spell; the tergiversate wild king lion caught in a trapfall net, his titubate tonicity guttural dry and thick-tongued.

Forewarned stress led great seething augur alacrity so that Amii ran around, sitting on the floor to face her son. "Elijah!"--she called to him, leaning to grasp his arms. He dug his nails into her arms as she instinctively pulled away from him. "I want to go Home!"--he screamed and moaned at the same time, wide eyed wild, then his head dropped down to the floor, his eyes rolling back fluttering. Long red streaks of fingernail scratches on her arms only barely began to draw blood. Looking at the scratches on her arm, then up at her ex-husband she said, "Forgive me for what I am about to do, because I know it's going to look a little crazy."

"What?!"--asked Elijah's father nervously, "What are you about to do?"

Horror flowed tingling every nerve, knowing she must unequivocally posture the chattels stipulating her son's suffering and save him! Out of fear her son might commit hara-kiri she harboraged her love to be the guide. Amii placed the palm of her hand *compressed* onto Elijah's forehead. Looking directly, *intensely*, in his eyes she lovingly forcefully shouted-- "GET... OUT... OF... HIS... BODY!" Miraculum was completely surprised that Amii might even suspect that he was in Elijah's body. Did she know? This surprise showed on Elijah's face. Suddenly it was as if Miraculum had been catapulted out of Elijah's body; he was tossed backwards up into the air with an incredible force. Miraculum fell from the air down onto his backside on the floor where he just stayed there, his mouth open, his eyes wide, feeling totally stunned and surprised.

Elijah lifted up to look at his mother asking with foggy confusion, "What happened Mom?" He lay down against

the floor, "I'm exhausted." Amii
gathered Elijah into her arms, cradling
him, rocking him. She kissed his head.
His father wiped the sweaty hair from
Elijah's forehead. Exhaustedly drained
the child closed his eyes and sighed
against the cozy shoulder of his mother.
Oddly the boy fell quickly into slain
soporific sleep as if called by Morpheus
into the arms of singing mermaids near
warm-water hazy cliffs. Elijah's father
lifted his slumbering son out of Amii's
arms to carry him into his bedroom;
which was the second medium-sized
bedroom. Placing his son on his bed,
taking off the little socks Elijah had been
wearing, pulling the covers up to the
boy's shoulders. Leaving the room with
the light still on, he closed the door
behind him. Amii stood there in the
hallway shaking as he walked up to her;
the two of them embraced in a hug and
Elijah's father said, "I think I better go
now." Amii nodded her head still feeling
perplexed into a near lack of all thought

at all; walking beside her ex-husband as if sleep-walking to the front door which he silently exited. Amii locked the door behind him then turning around she laced her fingers to fret mosaic until at last her brain could think of *something*. There was a pile of dirty clothes that needed cleaning, it was the first and only thing she could muster into thought at the moment.

Padding half dazed into the garage, opening the lid of the washing machine, she reached into a plastic basket on the floor to pick up an arm-full of some dirty laundry which she tossed still absently and nervously into the washing machine. Amii jumped, letting out a startled scream when one of Elijah's toys began to talk telling a nursery rhyme! It was the talking toy bear that had pads on it's feet which absolutely had to be pressed down hard, very hard, to make it start talking. She turned around breathing hard while putting one hand on her heart.

"Oh!" She laughed, "Stop that! You're scaring me! Silly bear!" Amii walked over to pick up the talking teddy-bear as it finished saying it's nursery rhyme. Examining the bear quizzically she quipped out loud: "I get it, you're a child ghost." Giggling half heartedly the nonplussed mother tossed the talking teddy-bear back down into the toy bin.

As she began to walk back towards the washing machine the toy train that lay in her path turned on it's lights and blinked. Amii jumped, chest pounding again. It's horn tooted; it's little wheels spun around so that it began moving across the floor! Amii fell to her knees, angrily grabbing the toy train (which immediately turned itself off!) Amii turned the toy train around her hands questioning it with incredulous quibble. Her blood quickened as she grieved, "Wait a minute… Elijah hasn't played with this toy in forever." Pulling the back plastic cover off of it she gasped to see that it didn't even have any batteries in it! Amii dropped the toy train as if it had been a scorpion.

A wind gushed past her skin, teasing the hair on her forearms. She stood up, turning in the direction of this flow of thick air. Miraculum was in the garage with his hands back against the corner of the ceiling with his knees pulled up and his arms crossed over them. As Amii looked up into that same corner she suddenly saw an ashen-skinned little boy with his legs up and his arms crossed and looking very angry. Sucking in a sudden disbelieving thrust of air into her lungs she almost panicked. Then the image was gone, but although the corner next to the ceiling looked empty, she knew with grappling gravamen that there really was a child ghost there. Intuitive flooding images with powerful tingling senses overcame her. She closed her eyes to bow her head, pressing one hand over her heart, the other hand covering her eyes.

Attempting to breath normally Amii sadly sighed saying, "You were murdered, weren't you." Dropped hands to her sides now, Amii's eyes darted to see the shovel hanging upon two nails against the wall.

Turning from the garage Amii ran outdoors into the backyard where she stopped at the blue pole sticking up out of the ground. Something inside her felt 'this is the spot' that somehow 'the boy's body might be buried here.' The whole thing seemed perfectly absurd but she had to know! Thus running back indoors through the kitchen to stand once more in the garage, she hesitated only a dab, before grabbing the shovel with her damp hands and sprinting back outside to the place of ground where the blue pole mounted dusty. Amii snapped the edge of the shovel into the dirt, pulling with all her might, pitching up clods of earth. Just this small effort made her sweat. Determinedly lifting the shovel, jabbing into the ground repeatedly. Amii's jolted quivering countenance nearly fell down flat when the ghost-child appeared before her!

Demanding shrilly, "Put it back!", the ghost-child cried. The shock caused her to drop the shovel, falling back against the grass onto her bottom and right elbow; she didn't even feel the certain pain of the drop. "Put back my bones!"-- required the ghost-child! Amii heard a sizzling sound like seven-hundred-and seventy-seven rattle-snake tails shaking.

The grass felt dewy damp like sticky sweat. Hardly believing what she was actually seeing, a smell of minerals and ozone swirled throughout her nostrils; a taste of metal filled the spittle in her mouth. "Put back my bones!"— commanded the child ghost more vehemently. Amii scrambled to her knees, pushing the upturned clods of dirt back in place, she patted it down. "There, there;" she said soothingly, "All back." The little ghost flew past her through the house door, fading away as he did. She couldn't even believe this was happening! Amii jumped up! She ran into the house locking the back door behind her. Scurrying over to the sink she frantically turned on the water, squirted some soap into her palm, scrubbing dirt off her hands then splashing water across her feverish face, whispering out loud in hopes that the ghost-child would hear her. "Why don't you let me help you? I could call the police, find you a good grave site and maybe you'd have some peace." Amii turned off the water to then reach for the hand-towel but before she could dry her hands or face the ghost appeared and shouted: "YOU DON'T UNDERSTAND!" Amii almost fell at the sight and sound, yet managed to grab hold of the edge of the sink and catch herself. Looking at the child apparition her heart filled with pity, becoming deeper a mother than even before. She sat down on the kitchen floor to speak gently to him. Lips parting Amii did not get a word in edge-wise. The spirit child tightened his fists at his sides anguishing, "I'm trapped here! Trapped! If you take my body somewhere else, I might be trapped *there*! I like this house!" He leaned in towards her, "I like this house!" Then the ghost-child flew past Amii straight through the wall leading to the garage! What Amii did not see was Miraculum fly through the garage, through the attic, and down into Elijah's room.

Miraculum woke the boy and asked him to play with him. Amii sat on the kitchen floor for a long time trying to figure out what to do. Finally she stood, taking a very tall plastic cup from the cupboard. Filling the cup to the brim with purified water from the plastic two-gallon container with a little spout at the bottom; drinking down the entire cup of water. Setting the cup on the counter a bit harder than she meant too she concentrated on breathing slower; easier. Standing there for a while racking her mind trying to think of a solution she sucked in air to blow it back out slowly. Suddenly Amii had an awkward unpleasant sensation that she had better check on Elijah. Walking out of the kitchen and through the hall to the door of Elijah's medium-sized room, she opened the door and was cut short from passing into the room any farther by a thin strand of white rope that pressed against her thighs. Amii looked down at the rope which prevented her from entering the room. Following the rope with her eyes she looked up around the room to see a perfect web like a spider's web intricately woven across the bedroom. The spider-web concoction was on Elijah, arm's-length just above his head. Elijah stood in the middle of this caveat intricate entanglement touching it with his fingertips; looking at it with awe.

Elijah murmured, "Oh what a tangled web we weave."

"*What*?!" Responded Amii incredulously terrorized. She looked at the flawless, spidery, elaborately intimate intricacy of it and stammered. "Wh..What are you.. doing honey?..Making a… spider's web?"

"Yes;" answered Elijah matter of fact as he touched lightly pampering it with his fingers.

"Where… Where did you get the rope, honey?" Amii followed the pirouette pinnacle with her eyes until she saw Elijah's kite next to his bed, its long string unwound. "Oh," she said with realization. "It's the kite string." Amii looked down at her son still speaking gently, "What made you do this sweetheart…*How* did you do this?"

Elijah pointed to the corner of his room saying stoically, "It was that little boy's idea."

Amii looked over at the corner and for a flash she saw the child-ghost. After a surmount of oxygen flushed through her lungs up into her throat, the corner looked empty. This time doubt be set aside, she knew the spirit was still there. Amii wagged her finger at the corner saying firmly: "That's enough! Nobody is allowed to harm my child, EVER!" Amii grabbed the webbed kite-string at her thighs, pulling at it hard and fast. Balling the string up until she had removed the 'stupid' web! She asked Elijah to follow her, which he did innocently compliant, thus together hand-in-hand they marched into the kitchen where she threw the ridiculous tangled ball of string into the trash-can. Picking Elijah up she sat him from her warm mothering arms to the living-room couch where she asked him to wait for her. Amii grabbed a pillow and blanket as well as several books from Elijah's room, too disgusted to be afraid to go back in; then back at the living-room couch she lay Elijah's head on the pillow; covered her son with the blanket. Feeling quasi queasy yet without fear now, she struggled quite perturbed over the young ghost's obvious influence to the absurd web thing! To think of her son so cruelly menaced completely ticked her off! How DARE he try to scare or harm her child! If she had been able to put aside her disbelief sooner, perhaps to think more clearly, then the small spirit could have just as soon come at her with centipedes dangling from his hair and fire shooting out of his eyes, while she simply stepped forward and slapped him hard across the face to stop him! He would have been in for a fight like he'd never known before, *with a Mom*! How dare he?

Elijah had no memory at all of the entire nights events, which was probably for the best. Except of course for the web thing. Yet her heart also went out to the child-ghost; she shook her head sighing. Smiling at her precious beloved,

Amii hugged her son tight and covered
his head and face with tiny kisses as she
said over and over, "I love you, I love
you, I love you." "I love you too, Mom,"
sweetened Elijah. Amii sat next to him
on the couch reading children's stories
until he fell asleep. His head on a pillow;
a blanket up to his shoulders. Then she
tip-toed into her bedroom and sat down
on the carpet in the middle of the room.

"You know" she said smoothly out
loud, "I scrubbed and scrubbed the carpet
in the closet of the third bedroom, and in
the pantry; the stains wouldn't come out
and looked undoubtedly like old dried
blood. When I pulled up the carpet in the
closet, there were bloody looking stains
in the wood underneath! I had to replace
the carpet in the closet and I put shelving
liner on the floor of the pantry." Amii
paused a moment to glance about the
room before continuing. "I wondered
why there was a lock on the outside of
the closet door." She took in a breath but

kept it up hoping to draw out the ghost. She knew in her gut he would come to her. "Now let me guess." An intuition came into her mind. "Your name is... Mmm... MMM... Mmm... Michael!" Suddenly the ghost-child appeared at the corner of the door with little sparkles of light behind him! Amii delved into staying calm.

He was angry no more; "You're reading my mind!"--he said.

"No, no," stated Amii, "It's simply an impression. Am I right? Is it Michael?"

"M-maybe," he said stepping closer to her.

"Look Michael, what happened to you is wrong. It doesn't matter what type of soul you are, nobody should be made to suffer such torture. You were just a child!"

"What do you mean what type of soul I am?" Miraculum stopped in his tracks

and looking down at himself was
annoyed to see that he was still in his
child's body image as Michael. He
stomped his foot just like a frustrated
child.. "Just a minute," lifting up a
finger. Turning around he walked back
to the doorframe; disappearing into small
sparkles of light as he walked straight
into it. Gone for a moment, then re-
appearing in a grown-up body form of
himself as Michael. He leaned against
the other side of the door-frame, grinning
smoothly from one side of his mouth
trying to look suave.

"Oh!"--exclaimed Amii sweetly, "I
see you're wearing a grown-up Michael's
body." She smiled a swaddling
genuinely ambrosial expression in his
direction.

"WHAT?!" Miraculum hooted. He
waved his hand at the door frame
whereby a large ornate full-body mirror
appeared. Looking into the mirror;
scrutinizing his own back, shoulders, and

also his hair which he ran his fingers through. He snorted unhappily then waved his hand so the mirror disappeared. "What... WHY!?" He hollered, childishly stomping that one foot again at the slight to his ego. So very annoyed to see himself still in a 'Michael' form; not his preferred form, Miraculum! Clearing his throat, composing himself, smiling at Amii he shrugged his shoulders. Then in his attractively handsome grown-up Michael-body he leaned one shoulder against the door-frame, trying once again to look suave; debonair!

"I know you miss your own kind," Amii proffered, "And I call upon your angels and guides. Even *my own* angels and guides, to take you into the light. Go to the light; go be with your friends and be happy. *Go Home.*"

"Ah!," excited Miraculum whilst he pointed at something to the side of Amii. She looked around the room in response to his gesture. Miraculum could tell she saw nothing. Yet it was Nnema! It was Nnema standing there! Nnema walking forward to take hold of Miraculum's hand. Miraculum with arm out-stretched, clenching Nnema's hand, looked back over his shoulder at Amii. A terribly worried expression crossed his face. *Miraculum pointed in a circle across his own face and said to Amii-- "You've got a...You have a..."*

Alas Nnema tugged at Miraculum to keep on walking, thus Miraculum turned away from Amii, letting Nnema lead him by the hand into a large white light that was shining to the side of the door-frame. Amii watched Michael walk away with his arms oddly stretched out. He disappeared into a bursting bright light that was off to the side. Smiling happily she felt sweat running down her neck and scratched at it. Then she felt her nose running; instinctively she rubbed her nose with the back of her hand. Yet when she looked down at her hand she was surprised to see blood! Amii ran into the small half-bath that was in her bedroom to look in the mirror. She was temporarily taken back to see that her nose and both of her ears were bleeding! The blood trickled rose-red down her neck from her ears; down the front of her face from her nostrils. Noting to herself that astonishingly she felt no pain. Amii washed her face and neck with soap and water, then stuffed toilet paper in her ears and nose. The bleeding, however, seemed to have stopped just as quickly as it had begun.

Miraculum; however, would soon find himself bellowing: "Bonsai!-eeeeee- eee-eee-eeeeee!"

TWELVE

Miraculum allowed Nnema to lead him into the bright side-light, where once again he found himself next to a lovely table beside two chairs in a meadow full of an array of beautiful perfumed flowers. Hence, where there should have been horizon there was simply white light all around them; above where sky ought be arched a dome of light. Miraculum looked magnificently joyful at his hands, arms, and shoulders; feeling of his curling horns. Hooraying grateful pleasure, "Yes!", he swelled loudly to find himself back in his true preferred form. He beat on his chest happily. (In case there is any curiosity, the answer is no, Demons

of his particular kind do not have nipples
on their chests!) Miraculum was so
fabulously overjoyed he fell innocently
into a ridiculously silly 'happy dance',
grinning wide! He also saw that he was
wearing his favorite prized leather pants
and boots. "I feel so much better!"—he
roared enthralled. With riveting peels of
laughter Miraculum strode over to
Nnema, then quite to the old man's
surprise, he gave the old wizard a huge
squishing bear-hug. He spun Nnema in a
circle under his arm! Miraculum then
mussed the long white hair on top of
Nnema's head as if the wizardly being
were a little boy. Nnema squinted one
eye, then merely shook his head and
chuckled, setting his hair back in place
with a quick run of his fingers. "Well,"
said Nnema placidly, "I'm glad to see
you are happy."

Looking over the edge of the meadow
Miraculum saw the perplexity of three
tall rectangular doors of white light

rushed abundantly by swirling strands of rainbow colors. Miraculum walked near to the three doors until he got about two feet away, whereby he baby-stepped another foot closer to peer at the mesmerizing doors with extreme high caution as if frightened he might accidentally fall into one. Gently Miraculum pulled away to baby-step backwards a couple of feet; staring at the doors feeling a tingling sensation of 'déjà vu'! Nnema strode over to stand beside him while Miraculum scratched at his spine, skull, and ears where the tingling sensation crawled his skin the strongest. "What... are they?"—Miraculum queried.

Nnema moseyed over to the doors; putting a hand in front of the first one. "This first door will take you Home." Taking a few small steps he placed a hand before the second door. "Hmm, yes, this second door will take you back to Amii's side."

"Well I don't want *that*." Like a disturbed dandy Miraculum continued to scratch himself against the déjà vu creepy-crawlies. "I think I need some wine!" (Scratch, scratch.) *"Lots and lots of wine!"*

"I fully appreciate your sentiments." Stepping forward Nnema hovered his hand in front of the third door. Lifting one nostril, squinting his eyes, he pulled his hand away quickly to tap his fingers meditatively in deep thought. "Hmmn;" noised Nnema.

"What do you mean? What does 'Hmmn' mean?" Miraculum bounced softly and nervously from one leather booted foot to the other. "What is it?"

Nnema set his palm back in front of the third door squinting his eyes, furrowing his brow with concerned concentration. Shaking his head in perplexed grandiosity Nnema allowed his arm to drop, then folding his arms together in front of his abdomen, walked back over to Miraculum's side. "I have absolutely no idea what's behind the third door." This was said with stagnant resignation.

"What?!"—snorted Miraculum indisposed. "How can that be? You are supposed to know everything!"

"Miraculum, it pains me to tell you, but sometimes things are a surprise. If a surprise is what you want."

"That... that's..."

"Ridiculous?"

"To say the least Sir!" Miraculum pulled his chin down against his neck while pressing his lips together; pushing away a little roll of nausea. He thought of his Michael lifetime and the aching ecstatic hours watching TV. "Ohhh, I get it. I've seen it on television! If I go through that third door I'll either win a million dollars, or I'll get a live baby donkey that I'll have to keep and brush it's fur, and have to feed hay or oats or some such thing."

"Donkey!"—Nnema blatted out, then began laughing uncontrollably uproariously.

"I've seen it! It's not so funny! Television game shows, you know, it is always a million dollars or a donkey behind the surprise door!"

Attempting to politely contain himself Nnema was struggling with laughter. Striding to the third rectangular door of light he roved his hand in front of it thoughtfully. "No, no," Nnema said, "I sense no donkey's here."

"Are you sure old man!?"

"Quite sure." Nnema stepped giggling back to Miraculum's side, putting a caring arm around him. He was trying to choke down the laughter bubbling up in him again.

"It's… it's… just that it is so… there's a word on the tip of my tongue here…"

"It is frustrating." Nnema finished Miraculum's sentence.

"Yes! I'm… I'm…"

"You are afraid of what might happen; or that you might get stuck."

"You're reading my mind!"—sorely exclaimed Miraculum! He *glared* one eye open and the other closed at Nnema!

"I'm not reading your mind. I *can't* actually read your mind. I can only know what you might be thinking or feeling or about to say, by imagining what I myself might think or feel or say if I were you and in your position. That's how that works." (Nnema was still burping back chuckles.)

"Well, *Weird Sir*, it is not…"

"Not funny?"—Nnema finished Miraculum's sentence.

"*STOP THAT!*" Miraculum set his jaw. Pursing his lips in angry frustrated exasperation. "That, *Strange Man*, is very, <u>*very*</u> annoying!"

Nnema pressed his hand over his mouth trying to quell his unwanted out of control laughter, mumbling sincerely, "So... so very sorry. Truly."

A thrilling mercurial surge of treasure-hunt intoxication employed him engirdled in a sudden captivating grip. Energy immersed Miraculum so reverently he began to bounce up and down. "I have FAITH!"—he roared while muscling his arms.

"Oh dear." Nnema spoke a soft sobering concern; shaking his head left to right.

"I have *faith!*" Miraculum tensed all over in his fanatical roar!

"Please, son, please…" Nnema aimed for eye contact with Miraculum. Placing his hands on Miraculum's shoulders he jerked the seeming monster in a turn so hard that the creature looked directly into Nnema's eyes. "Take my advice. *Go Home.*"

Miraculum walked back to the edge of the table; placed his hands on it's smooth corner to steady himself as if he were a runner about to jolt off into lightening sprint. He snuffed in and out air from his nostrils several times. Slowly taking both arms into stretching movements of thick fists lifting from one hip down to the other hip. Instant exquisitely immaculate wide-pounding movements of his throbbed legs as he ran excathedra forward! Miraculum jumped through the *third* door shouting: "BONSAI!"

THIRTEEN

Miraculum landed from his bonsai-screeching fall in a straddled position with his hands fisted, his arms pulled up close to him, his head down, his eyes closed tightly. He heard muttering and what sounded like cars honking. Tentatively opening his eyes to look up, he placed the back of one hand over his eyes in temporary blinded confusion until he realized that the bright light before him was the *sun*! Miraculum looked around with interest. He had landed on a busy sidewalk smack-dab in the middle of New York City! Someone behind Miraculum, a male voice said "Awwww!-Right! Major cool work, man!" Miraculum turned around to see a young couple whom both seemed very short to him. The young man had a ring through his nose, three rings through his bottom lip, his hair stood straight up, and the lobes of his ears each had two large wooden circles inside of them.

"You see me?" Miraculum asked.

"Oh, I see you man, all the way dude. I totally feel you man!"--nodded the young man who pounded his fist against his heart. (Miraculum put his hand on his own heart in response.) "I have never seen such great work!"

"Yeah!" said the girl standing close to her sweetheart. "How did you do all the skin? Is it all tattoo?"

"Did it hurt when they put the studs in your head?"--asked the young man. "Do you have to unscrew the horns and take them off just so you can sleep at night?"

"Uhhh..." Miraculum noised.

"Where did you get it done?" Inquired the girl. "Oh I know! I bet you had it done at 'I'm Invented Too Tattoo'! Am I right?"

"Uhmmm...." Miraculum noised whilst slowly shaking his head yes.

"Oh! I knew it!" The girl exclaimed this excitedly. "It's the best! Everybody says so. I want to have my ears done." She pinched and pulled at the top of one of her ears. "You know, I want to have them clipped to look like a fairies!"

"Hey! Look at this!"--Childlike excitement coursed in Miraculum's veins as the terrific idea of showing them his wings trussed through his mind. Squeezing; clenching his eyes and muscles; snorting inadvertently. (Nothing happened; not a single feather.) Before he could examine his shoulder blades a girl that to anyone else might have passed for a boy whom stood in an army jacket with long, gray baggy pants full of pockets hanging over her tennis shoes said, "Great muscle pose!"—and

handed him a dollar bill! "Thanks?"—
Miraculum hushed as he took the dollar
bill from her.

"Why don't we get some lunch, then
go check it out, the 'I'm Invented Too
Tattoo'?" The young man said this to his
girlfriend wrapping his arm around her
shoulders as he turned her around to face
the other direction. Looking back over
his shoulder to Miraculum he raised an
arm making a peace sign with his fingers.
"Stay cool, dude," he said to Miraculum,
then turned away sauntering off with his
lady. After a beat too long Miraculum
raised his arm up in the air making a
peace sign shouting, "Stay cool!" The
young man with his arm around his girl
kept walking, but turned around to look
at Miraculum for one moment wherein
he smiled and nodded.

*   *   *

Miraculum scanned his surroundings until his gaze landed over to a brick wall just steps to the left of the hot sidewalk where he was stood. He saw a most fabulous sight! Truly remarkable! A magnificent magnanimous sight that had him thrilling! Leaning against the speckled peckish brick wall beside a shop-door was a man whom Miraculum thought must be half snake! (How delightful!) Near the welcome sight was an equally beautiful image to behold! For up against the snake-like man was a woman who appeared to be part cheetah! (Yummy!) She had long silvery whiskers extruding from the puffs raised in her cheeks at either side of her nose! Her long dark hair was pulled back behind two *pointy folded ears*! The woman's body; covered from across her cheek-bones all the way down her throat, also completely covered her arms and the back of her hands, with what Miraculum did not know were *tattoos*. He thought these were real marks of a cheetah.

Looking down at the skin of the woman's legs showing between her boots and her shirt Miraculum saw that her legs too were covered in the marks of a great cheetah-cat. (Tasty! *Ravishing*.) Her eyes were light green with pupils like a cat. Miraculum walked right over to the couple with love-warmed happiness. "Are you a snake-man?" Miraculum asked this guy gleefully.

"No, man. I'm a lizard… Can't you tell?" Then the magnificent gentleman opened his mouth, stuck out his tongue (which was split down the middle) and he wriggled the two ends of his tongue up and down. Miraculum adored this man!

Miraculum sepulchered sincerely, "Hey! I have a friend who can do that!"

"Cool!"--nodded the lizard man. Covering his entire body over his face to his bald head were designed scallops… down his throat, chest, arms, everywhere! Small green tattooed 'scales' all over his skin. Poignantly he proudly pointed out the implants under his skin, "Look at this!" Implants bulged from under the skin of his face and scalp. "And this!" Implants under the skin of his forearms and wrists. Miraculum thought it was all real. He had no knowledge of implants or tattoo's. "We were just admiring your work!"--said lizard man. "It's beautiful! It's *flawless*!"

"Yup!" Acknowledged the cat-girl. "We were just saying you look magnificent. It's got to be some of the best work I've ever seen!" Cat-girl pinged her whiskers on one cheeked side with her thumb and middle finger. She had a very sweet, kind, playful Soul. "Look at this!" She opened her mouth to show Miraculum her fixed dental fangs.

"Oh! Me too!" Thrilled Miraculum then he leaned forward, opened his own mouth, raised his upper-lip with his fingers; showed her his molar fangs!

"Whoa!" Mistily the cat-girl awed true admiration, "Those are beautiful fangs!"

"Those are great, man!" Admiringly the lizard-man took a gander at Miraculum's fangs. (Miraculum felt so proud.)

"You both are 'great-man' too!" Smiled Miraculum, meaning every word without realizing the awkwardness of his speech. He wiggled his eyebrows at the cat-girl, picking up her hand delicately to kiss her knuckles. "And you my dear are gorgeous!" She batted her eyelashes at Miraculum, twirled a piece of her hair; giggled, blushed. Looking at lizard-man he smoothed, "You, lucky lizard, must always treat her as a precious gem!"

"She really is, isn't she." Proudly grinned lizard man; he leaned towards his girlfriend to kiss her tenderly, lovingly, upon the temple next to her hairline.

"Did you get your work done at the 'I'm Invented Too Tattoo'?" asked the cat-girl. "That's where we got our implants done. We work at a really cool freak-show; that's where we met... *and* fell in love." She giggled smiling, purring at lizard-man who chuckled and kissed her on the mouth softly. It was the second time Miraculum had heard that name (Tattoo-Too?); his curiosity caused his heart to pound hard and fast.

"Yes." Miraculum began, "The..I'm Invented Too Tattoo?... actually, I'm trying to find it... silly, I know. I just forget where I am and get lost so easily! Ha!" He tried to sound casual.

"Don't sweat it," said lizard man, "I do that all the time."

"So do I!" Chimed cat-girl.

"You're almost there." Lizard-man
continued, "Just at the end of the block
take a left."

"Ha! I knew it had to be close!"
Miraculum lied. Turning, he started
down the sidewalk.

"No! No!"--shouted lizard man "The
other way!" He pointed the opposite
direction. "The other way!"

Miraculum looked at him
dumbfounded for a second then waved
his hand at cat girl and lizard man with a
large silly smile saying, "Oh yeah!
Thanks!" Thus he turned himself around
to begin striding along the New York
City heat-smoldered sidewalk with a
mixture of curiosity, excitement, and
determination. Miraculum strode
happily, coming to the end of the block
he turned left, nearly running into a
business-man with slicked-back hair,
cabalistic gray suit, white shirt buttoned
up high to the tune of a maroon tie with

small gold circles on it. The business man swung his swarthy briefcase out to his side hitting a robust woman in the stomach whom was carrying a paper-bag of groceries in one hand, a sweetheart of a dusky dark small child whom was thankfully holding her hand on the other side opposite the swung briefcase. She straightened her light-blue pill-hat with it's petite bantam blue arid silk flowers on a stout lift of the same hand she carried the groceries in, saying to the businessman while she kept walking: "Watch out mister! What, are you trying to wallop my kid?"

"You see me?!" Miraculum asked this question in all sincerity of whether the businessman could actually see him. Of course the tailored man took Miraculum's request the wrong way saying, "Sorry." Then looking up higher to see Miraculum's face he said, "Yyyyyes... whatever show you work in, it's kind of hard *not* to see you."

Grabbing to shake the nape of his gold-specked maroon tie like he always did when he was nervous the man tucked his head down to turn around walking briskly away.

A cute Asian college student in a uniform-type outfit, a backpack on his shoulders that he flippantly fingered the straps with his thumbs, had seen the whole thing as he waited at the bus stop. Sensing the event being witness by the adorable short-haired student wearing his sweater-vest and trim jacket, Miraculum sauntered toward him grinning a zealous smile, beat his own thick chest one thump, saying: "*You* see me?" Nonplussed; in fact thinking Miraculum was magnificently interesting, the student smiled back giving an affirming thumbs up and said, "Outfit is rave!" Miraculum had no idea what 'rave' meant but he liked the sound of it. With great pendulous arms swinging he continued strolling down the noisy city sidewalk while looking up at business signs hung in chaotic mixtures of colors and writing along continuous buildings. A small Vietnamese food shop wafted smells like wolfs-bane and basil. Cars honked. A chow-chow dog barked from across the street as it tottered alongside it's owner until yanking the leash to squat, depositing a warm brown mush which the owner had already been prepared for with a plastic bag over her hand and a wanton tender loud proud vocalization of 'good, good dog.' There seemed no end to the whirling blending noises.

Startled to actually find the place Miraculum stopped in his tracks to stare over the psychedelic hand-painted sign with tiny blinking lights all around it that announced: 'I'm Invented Too Tattoo.' Deeply sucking in a lungful of encouraging air Miraculum bit his lower lip before opening the door of the tattoo establishment. He stopped the door midway to gaze up at the tinkling cowbell that rattled. Closing the door again slightly Miraculum eyed the cowbell which clinked once more to the doors movement. This was somehow very fun and implacably interesting so he grappled the door a bit to admire the cowbell rattle and tinkle once more. 'Hmmn'; Miraculum rumbled. Glaring up at the bell he pulled the door a teensy-weensy bit five more times to listen. Feeling finally satisfied he flung the door wide open with a slung hand behind him; stomping into the establishment. Passing the lobby while a girl in a 1940's style haircut and lipstick, a tiny fairy tattooed on her white neck, stood behind a register asking Miraculum, "May I help you? May I help you Sir?" Miraculum, honestly *so* distracted that he didn't even hear her simply walked straight onward into a room towards the back that attracted him due to practically gleaming with white surgical lights. Once he walked into the open room he saw a man with bright lamp lights on long poles glaring shiny down on his head amidst the fluorescent lights radiating from the ceiling. A bald man whom sat in a large torturous chair looked up at Miraculum with absolutely no expression at all despite this interruption of the procedure. Beside the bald man sitting was a tall skinny gentleman and a young woman; both wore surgical gloves. Skinny-man held the most peculiar looking metal instruments in his gloved hands. All he did was lift an eyebrow at Miraculum and smile. The woman was wide-eyed, open-mouthed, for merely an instant. Both went immediately back to what they were doing before the intrusion.

"Come to see my work, have you?" Skinny-man seemed proud to have someone come check out his fine art. Wearing his surgical gloves he stood a pillar bearing scars in hieroglyphic designs over face, arms; riddled by tattoos holding many stories. Looking down at the face of the bald man sitting

in chamberlains chair he asked quite
matter of fact his opinion of Miraculum's
presence. "You mind if he stays and
watches?"

"No. I'm down with it."
Chalcedonian response taken as a life-
affirming positive acceptance. His poor
bald head reddening whelped with spots
of blood.

"You've come to the right place."
Nodding her chin toward Miraculum the
woman spoke softly. "My man here is
the *best!*"

"Go ahead." Gesturing with his tools
in hand skinny-man shifted his eyes to a
white plastic chair against the wall near
the open door. As if given a command
Miraculum obediently sat down. "I don't
know who did your work but it's
fantastic! The horns are splendid! But
I'm telling you whoever he or she was,
don't go back to them. I'm the one you
want. And I'm very safe and careful

with my work. This is art, man.
Anything you want, practically anything,
I can design it and make it happen for
you. I'll bet you want more implants."

Now what amazed Miraculum was
during this entire time skinny-man
covered by hieroglyphic scars spoke to
him as if Miraculum's appearance were
perfectly normal. (He'd been screwing
metal spikes into the bald man's head!)
Spikes rolling perfectly upon some
implanted device under the guy's shaved
scalp. Nursingly the female dabbed
away blood while occasionally patting
the patients hand in loving
encouragement.

"What do you call that?" Miraculum
wanted to know.

The body artist smoothed a grin
across his face glancing over at
Miraculum while screwing down a spike.
"Body modification." Laughter softly
bubbled in his breath. "But you already

know that, don't you brother?"
Examining the spike; allowing the
woman to wipe away blood. "Any work
you want added, you come talk to *me*
first."

"Will do," stated Miraculum standing
up. For lack of what else to do he gave
the artist a soldier's salute then turned
briskly and walked right out of the tattoo
parlor.

Back out onto the busy noisy city
sidewalk Miraculum sauntered as if he
had purpose despite the fact that he truly
didn't know where he was walking too or
why. "Body modification," Miraculum
kept repeating to himself. "Body
modification." These words swirled
around in his mind. These were humans?
The lizard-man? The cat-woman? The
boy with metal rings in his face and
wooden circles in his ears? These were
humans!

As Miraculum looked up into the musty gray-blue sky seeing birds floating on the air, an airplane zooming past fluffed clouds to leave a string of white puffiness floating behind it; as his eyes soaked in the faces, bodies, and multi-colored garb worn on these human bodies he felt as if the knowledge of these humans and various other creatures of wings or feathers or fur or green-beetle sticky feet were marvelous miracles. "What miracles we all are!" Each stomping foot on the sidewalk that he heard, every cough or boom-box song, even the horns of cars, the sound of a siren far in the distance were music that prickled and tickled his eardrums. Music to the ears!

Miraculum halted to stand still watching a family of bobbing gray, black, brown, and white feathered pigeons that seemed to dance on their clawed feet just on top of an awning made of green polyester. The coos and trills of the pigeons were a fabulous song to hear. He especially loved how the pigeons turned away from the awning to flick their tails up and down and drop lovely splatting wet poo onto the ground, for he found the very idea of poo very humorous and therefore delightful. While he watched the smooth-feathered flicking tails and plopping white wetness that hit the ground and reveled in the vibrato tones from the birds throats, a tickle hit his tongue with a profoundly familiar taste. It was a rich meaty flavor he tasted from the air upon the tip of his taste-buds. Then the flavorsome taste hit in a tingling salty sensation upon the sides of his tongue.

It was only secondly that a waft of a most palatable scent of meaty spice flew in a ribbon of waves into his nostrils. Sniffing deeply he found relish in the sensation of the zesty gusto he was smelling. Turning with pleasure Miraculum followed the streaming

steamy smell to a small portable stand.
A short man in a bar-b-q red-striped
apron held tongs in his hand as he tapped
his fingers on a tray of red ketchup,
yellow mustard, white onions, and green
pickled pieces of some vegetable, that
was attached to his food stand. On the
sidewalk food stand there was a sign
which read: Tofu Dogs. "Tofu dogs!;"
exclaimed the man in the red-striped
apron to Miraculum. "Get a tofu dog,
sir! Made of the best soy-beans and
spices for the smoothest meatless tofu
hotdog you ever set your teeth into!
Mouth-watering delicious, guaranteed!"

"I'll have one!" Indeed Miraculum
could hardly wait to see if he could really
eat. Not to mention the savory tang
already on the tip and sides of his tongue.
The exquisite frenzy of scrumptious
smells filled his nose. He could hardly
wait to taste one!

"That'll be two dollars and fifty
cents," said the short food-stand man.

He halted to grasp a tofu hotdog in his tongs from the steaming bin when he heard Miraculum's response.

"Uhhh," Miraculum vocalized. Suddenly Miraculum knew exactly what to do about his lack of financial means. Backing up several long steps he then turned and walked back to a store near the green awning with the dancing pigeons, where a round man with a white paper hat on his head wearing a long white apron covering his chest down to his feet stood smoking a cigarette. "Hey!"—Miraculum spoke to the man in the white paper hat whom looked up at him to blow a plume of blue-gray smoke from the corner of his mouth. Miraculum searched for the right words only a moment, then it came to him: "Brother!" Stretching his hand out to the guy. "You got another smoke?"

"Yea, sure." The paper hat man said with a shrug of one shoulder with the cigarette between his teeth. Pulling a pack from his pocket he shook out a cigarette and gave it to Miraculum (who thanked him.) Stuffing the pack back into his pocket he slid out a lighter and cupping one hand around it flicked the thing into a medium-sized flame. Holding the cigarette awkwardly Miraculum leaned forward, placing the filter against his lips, setting the end of the cigarette into the flame. Breathing in deeply, an uncontrollable regurgitation of smoke came storming out of Miraculum's lungs so that he coughed! His cough was so violent he thought he might never catch his breath again. The man laughed watching. Yet with a raising of his arms up high Miraculum breathed normally again with just the meekest trailing of a hiccup.

"Thanks," he uttered again to the man in the white paper hat who was now frowning at him. Miraculum walked half-way back to the tofu hotdog stand where he stopped by a brick wall where a homeless man that smelled interestingly of dirt and halitosis sat with his bottom on the sidewalk and his back against the brick wall. His furry head and face were mosaic for his ruddy cheeks and yellowed blood-shot eyes. In his lap was a tattered gray blanket of some sloppy knitting, and in the center of the blanket was an old tin can. Miraculum leaned down to the homeless man, offering him the fresh smoking cigarette.

"Hey! Thank you. Bless you." The homeless man said this as he blinked against the assault of sunlight and happily took the cigarette from Miraculum.

Miraculum responded, "You're most welcome, Little Hobo."

"Hobo?!"—the man hooted in surprise and indignation.

Miraculum swiped the homeless man's tin can up so quickly it was practically a ninja move. He poured nearly fifteen dollars of bills and change into his large hand, dropped the can back into the homeless man's lap gently, then kindly *patted the homeless man on top of his head.* He was already up and moving away when the shaking man yelled in an angry tone: "Hey!" He watched Miraculum walk off; shrugged his shoulders, steadied his shaking fingers, looked at his cigarette with lowered eyelids to contentedly smoke and enjoy it.

Miraculum tromped his way back to the man in the red-striped apron beside the sidewalk food stand whereby he bought two tofu dogs. Putting red ketchup, yellow mustard, green pickled things, on both of them simply because he could. With gentlemanly manners, his pinkie in the air, he slowly, sweetly took two elegant bites chewing one bite laggardly after the other to his immense fulfilling joy! Overcome by a magnificent feeling of serendipity, eyes wide with delight, he stuffed the last of his first dog into his mouth nearly whole and chewed in open chomping childish jolly at the grand flavor filling not just the tip and sides of his tongue but the middle and far back of his tongue also with a spice of pungent depth.

"Kismet," growled Miraculum gleefully as he handed the other tofu dog to the homeless man while hardly even looking down as he walked past. The homeless man gestured with the hand holding his tofu dog, and in a hoarse voice he intoned with renewed indignation, shouting after Miraculum, "*Hey*! Horn-head guy! You put too much *green stuff* on this dog! What makes you think I want a bunch of pickle-dee-dee-dee green stuff on it?!"

FOURTEEN

Miraculum felt happy he'd given the homeless man the hotdog as he continued walking until he'd walked half the block whereby he turned back the other direction, nearly walking past a gorgeous phenomenon he couldn't believe he'd nearly missed! In a huge salmon colored clay pot was a lush unusual tree-like swirling vine of engorged green leaves holding bright orange magnificently healthy flowers called: *Trumpets*. They held an abundant clean perfume. Miraculum's very spirit had a scent to it that smelled faintly of rich red roses mixed with bright orange cannas. *Everyone has a scent*, yet this was not a scent he particularly noticed about himself. Miraculum had a friend, a family member, back in his Heaven...his Home... the friend Grolin whom smelled softly of raw cashews and yellow curry.

Another brethren of his, Juansa, smelled tentatively of burned paper, violets, and skunk spray. Yet none of his family felt specifically aware of their own smell. It all just seemed a marveling mysterious mixture of scent when they were all together that they simply found, well, like happiness.

When it came to smells they were deeply enamored with, all of his kind enjoyed that which smelled something like rot that boiled out of human bowels. Not that the smell was so fabulous or pleasant, but that the *playfulness* of the stink was *enjoyable*! They could play games with the smell which they threw at one another with divine hilarity; so much fun, quite like humans playing a game of paint ball. Miraculum stuck his nose all the way down into one of the Trumpet flowers; snuffling long, as fully as possible, enjoying the soapy clean mint-hinted perfume. Closing his eyes to behold the perfumery in all it's glory, his eyes popped *open* suddenly in a fabulous surprise as he sneezed with his nose still buried *in* the Trumpet flower! Trumpet petals jiggling and echoing the sneeze before folding it's silky petals back around his nose. He laughed whole-heartedly, pulling his head away as he fell into a fit of giggles. Touching the thick leaves of lime and forest-green. They felt resilient yet squishy at the same time in his fingers. Rolling his hands around the Trumpets velvet smooth touch; rubbing the petals gently across his palms, fingertips, wrists, and the back of his hands! The sensation of pure scented touch soaked into the pores of his skin until he could feel the fluffiness of tactile sensitivity enter each distinctive nerve receptor to communicate a sparkling blanket of pure and tangible contact. To smell, to touch; to *feel*!

Winding his way around the glowering Trumpets that dripped a wet moisture upon his fingertips, he looked and *savored* the shimmered watery-like *gold* color as he came to the other side of the plant. His eyes enjoyed seeing the delicate vision of strong greenery betwixt gentle petals! Upon the window pane of the store-front next to the Trumpets was a poster he now saw. Smiling still from the Trumpets perfume Miraculum's eyes watered when he absently glanced at the store-front window. He saw the picture on the poster. It was a *donkey*! "*Aaack*!!" --Miraculum accidentally yelped, jumping backwards when he saw the donkey! (The animal sported some sort of coffee.) Then with baby-steps he jimmied his way in one side-step after another keeping his eyes fixed on the poster of the donkey in a fearful stern frown. "Yikes!"—he whispered. His hands were grasping at the Trumpets gently as he suspiciously eyed the poster of the donkey until he heard the store's bell ring when a small-boned woman with little feet and long silky hair of Cherokee descent enter the convenience store. Drawn by the division-bell, between the outside world and the inside convenience establishment, Miraculum followed the woman inside.

The woman ordered a pack of cigarettes; paying in cash. She was so deep in her own thoughts she did not even seem to realize Miraculum was there as she sighed, turned away, leaving the store with her purchase. She smelled like sweat and baby-powder. The Trumpets outside the store were a gift to the owners by the wife's mother-in-law. It was an absurd gift for anyone living above their own store in a crowded pavement city like New York City. Yet for the man and wife it was a gift not to be taken lightly. They put it in front of the store in the large salmon-colored clay pot when it was still a young fledgling Trumpet. Then one day in the Trumpets mid-season during an unusually mild summer there was a most unusual sight to see! A tiny hummingbird not only showed up here in all places as no-one had ever seen before in the city but showed up flitting, sipping, and humming amongst the Trumpet flowers! Not only an amazing sight to see the itty-bitty hummingbird drink upon the nectar, but the hummingbird (a very gentle and sensitive creature of constant movement) actually stopped to land; sitting still! Preciously petite this hummingbird whom exists on sweetness and beauty, actually nested in the Trumpets; coming out to sip the sweet honey-like drips before resting to watch as people occasionally noticed it. Usually the hummingbird so small and rare was like the lovely wall-flower with nectar dripping like it's tears as it sings a melodious tune beyond the realm of human hearing. Of course the man and wife whom owned the convenience store saw the hummingbird as a good luck sign.

Miraculum happily slammed both hands upon the store's front counter; he'd thought the Trumpets as a sign, and he asked the couple what he thought would induce a compound magnificent new brilliant idea. The wife was full flossed with beauty even in her older age, as was the husband nearly her own age. They had an arranged marriage although they'd known each other since childhood. With deep respect, honesty, and pure faithfulness to one another, they were a lucky pair. The wife wore a sparkly sari with a blue sash across her shoulder pinned at the waist by a sparkling butterfly gem of a broach. The husband had a bejeweled shirt in patterns of green and white up to a v-neckline and falling past his waist. Each had a red dot on their forehead; although the woman's red dot appeared more ornate. "And how can I be helping you today?"—asked the husband.

"I want a doctor for the… bean?" Miraculum pointed to his head. He was having trouble finding the correct word.

"For the bean?" The male store owner wanted to help his customer, but this was most confusing!

"No!" Miraculum tapped his head; searched his mind.

"Oh! Oh!" The wife thought she understood now. "Bean-*no*! He wants the medicine. For the stomach pains."

"Oh yes!" Now the husband understood (so he thought.) "He has the gas!"—he said to his wife, "He wants the Bean-*no*, for the gas."

"No, no, no." Miraculum shook his head frustrated.

"I am so sorry to inform you Sir," the male store owner seemed truly sad, "but

we do *not* be having the Bean-*no* in our
store."

"I don't have gas!" Miraculum's
frustration surmounted. He pointed to
his skull again. "The... the... nut?"

The husband was trying very hard to
help Miraculum and please another
valued customer. "You be wanting the
peanuts?"

"Not peanut," frowned Miraculum
poking at his head.

"Oh!" The wife tapped her husband's
arm; she too was meticulously attempting
to be helpful to their customer. "He
means the head! The head!"

"The head?"—queried the husband.
"Now I get it, of course, you must to be
having a *headache*. Many is our
selection; I will show you here.."

"A doctor!"—blurted Miraculum;
suddenly the word came to him and he
shouted it a little too loudly in his

excitement. "Therapist!" Smiling now, wagging a finger at the couple. "Therapist! Like I saw Amii go too; a head doctor."

"Aim me?" Husband confused turned his eyes in a worried glance to his wife.

"Yes, yes! I *have* to got it!" Sudden exultant intuition had come to the wife. "He means to say Dearest, for to want a doctor, for the head!"

Lighting up with understanding the husband grinned momentarily while nodding vigorously. "Yes! Oh yes!" Looking at Miraculum: "We do *not* be having one of those here Sir." Gesturing in a wide open span of his arm, he looked across his place. "We are to be meaning for to be a store. What you want, yes, is to be called a.. a.." Placing his hand on his wife's back he looked at her imploringly. "What is the word, my Love?"

"A psychiatrist!" She pointed a finger in the air with triumph. "I have it here for you Sir." She turned away to bend down behind a table against the wall where incense of sweet jasmine burned. Back to the counter she brought forth a large phone directory. Laying the telephone directory down in a thump, she and her husband looked at it; flipping through pages while Miraculum watched with great interest. "Here, here, it is." Apparently finding what they were searching for she turned the phone book around to face their customer. Miraculum glowered at it as the couple waited patiently, sharing a loving triumphant smile with one another.

Miraculum gazed at two pages of either side of the telephone directory that had been placed to the psychiatric business pages. He saw a series of doctor's names he liked quite a lot on the right-side page. Holding the left-side of the phone directory down with his left palm, swiftly, perfectly, almost seamlessly, he ripped the right-side page smack out of the directory! The couple both dropped their jaws in surprise while they watched this unconscionable act. Miraculum smiled at them: "Thank you! It's perfect!" Feeling somehow immediately self-conscious Miraculum for lack of a better thought on what to do decided to wave at the confounded couple, smiling at them ridiculously just as he had seen Amii do once upon a time when she'd been on stage. Miraculum pushed the door open to leave the store in this manner of behavior while holding tight to the torn out page. Outside he leaned in toward a lovely orange flower and with a rumble-chuckle of pleasure kissed the Trumpet on it's tender petal.

Inside the store the wife bobbled her head as she sadly said, "That man has deflowered our telephone directory."

In turn the husband also bobbled his head, then to steady his chin into stillness he cleared his throat. As the couple both stared down at the torn directory the man somberly acknowledged, "Yes. It is most unfortunate."

Miraculum looking up at the sky admiringly had walked only a few feet away from the convenience store when he nearly slammed head-on into the door of a café that was accidentally pushed too hard by the customer exiting. Stopping to blink he then decided to enter this café that had almost so rudely beaned him. Walking in with curiosity he looked around at the people inside while striding absently up to stand behind a woman whom was making a purchase at the cash register. Near the register was a glass encasement showing off a variety of quickly gained tasty foods. In front of Miraculum stood a woman in a business-suit skirt, silk shirt, and medium heeled pumps on her feet. She ordered coffee (black) and a slice of cheesecake. Served to her in a fast efficient manner,

Miraculum awed as he saw them let her
pay for it with a small plastic card that
the waitress swiped through a slit on a
box that was attached to the register by a
black cord. The business woman walked
away with her order. Miraculum stepped
forward and because he didn't know
what else to say, he ordered the exact
same thing—"I'll have a coffee. Black.
And a slice of cheesecake." He was
smiling like an idiot.

He too was efficiently served with a
slice of New York style cheesecake on a
small cream-colored plate; the cup of
black coffee in blue-striped Styrofoam
with a little white plastic lid on it; steam
escaping from a tiny hole in the top of
the lid. A plastic fork was the only
adornment next to the cheesecake on the
plate. Miraculum was fond of the bills of
money he pulled out from his pocket,
spilling it onto the counter. Snatching up
the bills because of this fondness he left
the waitress with undisguised disgust to

count through the mound of coins.
Scouringly grimaced he folded the torn-
out telephone page into a divinely
perfectly even square that he tucked into
safety by sliding it into his back pocket.
Miraculum waited for the waitress to
count, tapping a finger on the glass
counter; looking around the cafe. The
brown and white tile floor was fake;
white walls had been sponged over with
a watered-down paint of light sky blue.
People of every skin color, a wild range
of clothing styles, sat eating and talking,
reading, sipping, or alone snacking.
From the far end of the counter on the
tiled floor next to the wall a small gray-
white mouse with a long pink tail
crawled on it's little paws before
stopping to sniff the floor. Miraculum
excited upon seeing the mouse, squinting
his eyes with an overpowering urge to
grab hold of the piddling petite prittle-
prattling rodent. Yet with the strength of
a fortifying voluminous inward breath he
looked up at the menu on the wall to

restrain himself. This seemed to work very well. Then within only a moments ticking time he had to look at the mouse again. Just a peek.

Upon looking once again at the mouse he snorted through his nostrils yet maintained reserve. Glancing back up to the wall menu Miraculum grunted. Now all his fingers were tapping the glass counter; which the busied waitress took as a sign of indignance causing her to more slowly take her time in counting coins. Miraculum couldn't stand it, he had to see the mouse again, so he looked at the rodent wondering what the furry tyke was up too. *It was unthinkable what he saw*! The softly furred grayish mouse lifted it's front arms into the air, folding it's pink hand-like paws slightly. The rodent wriggled it's nose while looking Miraculum directly in the eyes! This mouse actually flicked it's whiskers at Miraculum! Oh, no doubt about it. This was a clear challenge for a chase!

Squeeking like a holler of alarm, eyes widening, whiskers and head pulling up, the mouse watched aghast as Miraculum rose into the air in one supreme inhuman leap, his knees and elbows bent with his fingers splayed, his back arched! Miraculum was across the room, hunched over with the mouse in his hands, within an *instant*! "Ha! Ha! Gotcha' little booger!" Suddenly without warning something caused Miraculum to feel a wave of self-consciousness that gurgled up from the pit of his stomach; froze him in position as the entire café fell quiet. Not a tinkle of a fork upon a plate; not a clunking spoon in a cup; not a cough or whisper, nor even the high-pitched screech of cutlery sounded out. Complete silence! Miraculum's eyes popped up to see everyone in the café staring at him.

Standing swiftly onto his feet, Miraculum smiled widely like a little boy, stretching his arms out before him.

Showing off to the café people the mouse
in his hands. He said, "I got it!" Many
people clapped; a few people shouted
'Yay!' Pausing, he acknowledged his
right to receive the clapping honors.
Raising one eyebrow proudly he also
bowed like a true dandy. Miraculum
turned after this fine moment; he walked
towards the register with his arms held
out straight before him; the little mouse
poking out it's eyes and nose from
between Miraculum's cupped hands.
The café patrons went back to their own
business. People once again were
speaking, eating, making noisy sounds of
knives on plates, forks plunking metallic.
Miraculum shoved the rodent into the
chest of the shocked coin-counting
waitress whose quivering hands
inadvertently grasped the mouse. She
squeaked and squealed, shakingly
pushing the mouse into the young male
waiters arms whom was standing next to
her with his mouth jaw-dropped
gawking. Sheltering the mouse in his

small hands the young male waiter had all disgust melt away when he looked down to see the rodent licking it's paw before scratching it's fluffy fur shoulder. He said, "Awwww."

Miraculum reached into his front pants pocket retrieving a dollar bill, asking the grossed out waitress: "Do I owe you more? How much do I owe you?" Running over to the huge bottle of antibacterial gel the waitress spurted five massive globs of the stuff into her palm, rubbing the goo while much of it dripped onto the floor; covering the gel across her hands, arms, and elbows in quick short high pitched noises: "Ooo, ewe-ewe, oooooo!"

"How much?!" Miraculum held out the dollar bill in his grasp.

"No, no!" Screeched the waitress continuing to scrub antibacterial gel into her skin. "You're *good*. It's fine. You got it! Just *take it*!"

"Ohhhhh…," purred Miraculum as his eyes took a gander of black coffee steaming forth from the secured white lid's tiny hole, the thick yummy cheesecake treat with gleaming silvery fork next to it. "Mmmm," he noised while taking the food and drink in hand; smelling of it as he went to sit down at a small square yellow-tinted table settled second from a table near the window. Placing his treats on the table, pulling the torn phone book page from his back pocket. Unfolding it from it's perfect square quite carefully. Pressing it down to smooth out any wrinkles. He read the list of psychiatrists whilst pipping the white lid off his coffee with his thumb, bringing the heated drink to his lips. Miraculum swigged a big gulp of it into his mouth before instantly managing the most beautiful spit-take ever to be recorded in history. Miraculum spewed the black coffee in spittled streams all over the table! It was gorgeous!

Tucking her chin, looking at
Miraculum with lowered eyes, and
chuckling hard, the blonde blue-eyed girl
sitting at the table beside the window
across from him said, "Careful there. It's
hot."

"Yes"—murmured Miraculum
experiencing a combination of hilarity
and embarrassment. Setting the hot
coffee onto the table he replaced the
plastic lid firmly. He wasn't going to
drink any more of it. It occurred to him
he should offer it to the blonde-headed
smirking girl. "Would you like to have
it?" (Offering the Styrofoam cup to her.)
She would have recoiled but it *was too
funny*, so she shook her head 'no' in a
tight-lipped smile, going back then to
eating her eggs over easy; turning away
to stare out the window. Now for the rest
of her meal she anticipated continuing to
stare out the window. Miraculum wiped
a spot clean on the table with the back of
his arm to manifest prim dexterity laying

out the sheet of paper; dabbing it with a napkin. Fastidiously Miraculum pressed the phone book page down to help straighten out any more crease marks. Studying the list of psychiatrists, their telephone numbers, address's, Miraculum slid his fork into the cheesecake. Rolling the bite of food around his mouth with lips closed, he enjoyed the smooth feeling of cheesecake against the grainy graham-cracker crust. It was a flavor of sweetness with underlying tones of mild bitterness like slightly spoiled milk. He loved it! Lolling the course particles mixed in creamy aromatic bitter-sweet taste around his closed mouth before chewing it, he ate the delectable dessert while meaningfully studying this list of psychiatrists. Miraculum found a name and address he felt particularly fond of. Tapping the torn phone page the store owners had given him he suddenly flung his arm out towards the egg-eating girl at the table next to him. "Have you got a pen or pencil?!" He demanded this whilst gazing at her from under his eyebrows. She jumped.

The blonde snapped her head in his direction with a curious look of slight fear on her face (but it wasn't fear of Miraculum; it was fear for her pen!) "A pen?"—she timidly muttered. A pen!? She had only one pen... her *favorite* pen! She didn't like to have anyone even *touch* her favorite pen! Taken off guard she nevertheless uttered, "Um! Yea. Yes; just a second." Frowning when she turned to unzip her baroque-looking purse she'd had tucked up against her hip facing the window side. Extracting her marvelous pen she slowly made a leaning revolution in Miraculum's direction, offering it to him in angst.

"Thanks"—he said gratefully while looking deeply into her eyes embarrassing her. Next, turning the pen around between his fingers admiringly, he said: "Pretty." He lifted one eyebrow

in a side-glance in her direction. She
said not a word but kept looking
nervously intent upon her pen for every
beating second without even realizing
she was doing so! Miraculum sincerely
enjoyed the pen, covered as it was from
top to bottom in halved circles of shiny
multicolored glass beads. He circled the
name and address of the psychiatrist he
had chosen. Then he circled it again; and
again. Miraculum circled it until he
formed an unnecessarily deep dark ring
around it. When he handed the
bejeweled pen back to the girl (whom
hadn't taken her eyes off it) he nodded,
saying politely: "Appreciate it." She
nabbed her pen much more quickly than
she meant too, then turned to quickly
stuff it into her purse. Out of some
deeper need to protect her precious pen
from others she took hold of the purses
shoulder-strap to tuck it with her fingers
underneath her thigh so she was sitting
on the strap! She placed her eyes
towards the window while dipping her

toast into the over easy eggs, taking big crunchy bites. A tiny humored smile returned to her face as she chewed, watching people walking outside on the sidewalk.

Miraculum stood up from the table after refolding , neatly tucking, the phone page; he grabbed the cup of coffee taking it with him. Marching out of the café he strode down the sidewalk with renewed firm intention. Pulling the torn page from his pocket he soaked in the address now and then while continuing to walk until he realized he'd passed that same homeless man whom apparently didn't like pickled relish, and held a dirty-gray knitted blanket in his lap; the Little Hobo that had smoked the gifted cigarette he'd given him. Halting, then stepping backwards until he was standing beside the hairy homeless halitosis gentleman sitting on the sidewalk. "Hey, Little Hobo! You stay cool man." Miraculum bending down handed the man his cup of coffee then emptied out all the rest of the monies from his pocket to throw it into the man's dusty lap. Without even bothering to see the homeless man's reaction Miraculum continued strolling in bright warm sunshine until he came to a stop at some street sign. Scrutinizing the street sign then gleaning in the address on the phone book sheet, Miraculum realized with loathing that he was going to have to do something horrible which he was sourly sore to undertake: ask for directions!

FIFTEEN

Aria da capo!—(And once again back in Dr. Roberts office, fully in the present moment, Miraculum sat on the couch completely quiet now that he had finished telling his story.) Dr. Roberts had heard his arguments in an often heated vigorous stance of debate regarding good, evil; existence. Listened to his dialectic controversy performing muscle poses for money in central park; sharing food with the same 'Little Hobo' he'd befriended. Nothing could prepare her for the story of his life as she'd just grimly parleyed audience too.

Dr. Roberts was stunned; she had been stunned from the moment he began telling his story and was stunned still!

She realized her mouth was hanging open so she shut it with an audible crunch of her teeth that was much harder than she'd meant it to be. Miraculum tossed the rococo pillow so that it fell carelessly at the end of the couch. He had no expression. Silence passed between patient and Doctor. Truly it was only approximately 46 seconds ticked away in consulate quiet yet to Dr. Roberts the silence seemed to last forever! Finally a morbid sly smile lifted one side of Miraculum's mouth.

Lifting his arm he pointed at a wood-framed photograph sitting on Dr. Roberts desk half facing him. "That's a lovely photograph. It's new, isn't it?" Then he said in a deep-toned hoarse almost hissing whisper, "Ammmii."

Snatching the photograph in some deeply embedded maternal instinct Dr. Amii Roberts pressed the frame against her solar plexus with the picture itself facing her somber professional suit jacket. "It's my son's wedding picture;" uttered Dr. Roberts, "He just got married."

"How nice," wisped Miraculum as he nodded his head in approval. "I mean it. Really. That positively *is* nice."

With a simple circle of a name he happened to be fond of, no-one could have been more surprised by the sheer bizarre happenstance of confounding coincidence than Miraculum was, to discover fate had brought him to Amii. The real Amii. *His Amii.* He wasn't even the one whom had chosen from the hysterically long, long list of psychiatrists; many pages of doctors available. Yet to open that particular page of the telephone directory; it was the convenience store owners that had opened it to such ironically weirdly spectral Moirai kismet of coincidence! As if the female beauty alongside her husband in the store had been the Greek goddess Mnemosyne herself come back to life from long-lost myth to execute the mnemonics of memory on the silver platter of a phone book! All to the unsuspecting *innocence* of Miraculum by the hand of *fate*! No indeed, no-one could have been more shocked than he, when he first entered her office and nearly fell to his knees upon recognizing her!

Dr. Roberts slowly, gradually, rose to her feet with a floaty dazed feeling tingling at the edges of her body. Never had she heard a description including her very own life's experience in such a detail undeniable and ghastly. Dr. Amii Roberts wrapped her hand around the plain black walking cane with the golden knob on top. Using the cane to aid her baby-sized steps, she hobbled around her desk to stand in front of it nauseously light-headed. She was so old now, she thought to herself. Miraculum stood. A cool, confident desire warmed the expression on his face. Feeling calm smooth confidence pulsing through him and beating in his heart in an electric flowing wave up into his shiny eyes. Languidly Miraculum strolled up to Amii. Walking to the right of her he gazed at her face, body, eyes, as if *smelling her*. As if she were still twenty years old in his eyes. Raising his hand to her hair Miraculum slow-flowingly pulled the bobby-pins out of Amii's donut-shaped bun, deliberately dropping the hair-pins onto the floor. He streamed his fingers lagging dragging through her hair so that Amii's long, aged pure-white hair flowed down across her shoulders and down her back. A strange electricity sparkled through Amii's spine. She watched him with surprised beaming eyes. Miraculum placed a strand of Amii's white hair at her forehead between two of his fingers; lovingly slicked her hair between his thickened fingers to gloss and smooth her hair around her face. She was shaking. Leaning in he whispered sincerely with his breath against her ear, "It's all about knowing. Isn't it Amii?" Pacing in slow steps to the other side of her. Whispering hot-breathed, lips upon her other ear, "Ammmii."

"You," she managed to speak, "you... your... you're a..."

"I'm a *Demon*." Miraculum stated this so calmly as he traced a finger through the white hair around her face most tenderly. Leaning inward closer he placed his fingertips under her chin so it was slightly gently lifted. "And you," he soothed with an almost seductive softness to his voice, "You are an Angel." Walking slowly to the other side of her body; so close to Amii that she could feel the heat rising off of him. "We're different, you and I," sweetly he whispered under his breath. "We're not the same." Miraculum sleekly ran the back of his knuckles in a lovingly smooth touch down her cheek, across her jaw.

"You know what you really are; don't you Amii?"

Her bottom lip began to tremble, her eyes became moist. "I've always known. But it doesn't even make sense in this world. I just... I just thought if I could help someone..."

Licentiously lank to breathily speak, his lips upon the superfluous flesh of her ear and cheek, his voice charming, wistful, "You wanted to save the world. Admit it."

"But there's nothing I can do"--Dr. Amii Roberts quivering voice. "So I thought... if I could just help one person... somewhere; somehow."

"You know what's funny?" Miraculum willow-whispered near her earlobe. "I...," he began, "I... wanted... to save... *you*." Miraculum pulled back to look at her. He smiled with the sympathetic compassion of a parent for a child they dearly cared about. Leaven bent to her face once more, he murmured, "That's funny; isn't it?"

"But I got so confused;" spoke Amii, "I got so confused by everything that happened in my life. Soul-scarring. Painful. Like a horrific immunization shot that wracks you with blisters; festers before it finally heals. It's still not completely healed; because it leaves a permanent scar. Permanent." Her naturally wine-colored lips trembled; her eyes stung.

"Will I remember all this when I get Home?" Miraculum asked sincerely, looking down at the floor while rubbing his chin; looking back up at her from under his eyebrows.

"Yes." She was breathless. "But you'll hardly ever think about it, and you won't feel anything about it. But... but you'll *Know*..."

"*Knowing*." Interrupted Miraculum. "That's what it's all about, isn't it?

Knowing *who you are*. And Knowing where you belong."

"Sometimes," the air caught in Amii's throat as she spoke, "Sometimes a message that is the most profound and important of all, is in fact very *simple...* so simple that you can't see the forest for the trees."

Miraculum pressed his face close to hers, his warmed exhalations wisped upon her prickled skin. His somatic breath scented odorous like fresh clean fragrant ginger. "'Evil' can not be allowed to hurt 'good'. And because there are so many kingdoms, you must keep them separated. It's all about Knowing."

Delicately Amii voiced sophic: "I just wanted to help. But; I can't." Licking her lips she staved away tears.

"You did help someone. Ammmii. You helped *me*."

Her head flung up suddenly, looking into his eyes astonished, demanding; she wet her bottom lip with a lick of her tongue. "How?! When?"

"I know who and what I am now." He kissed her quickly on the cheek.

Then with long strides of his gallant legs, hard steps of his feet, Miraculum began pacing. He yelled so harshly that Amii flinched, her muscles jumping. "There was a girl!"—he yelled.

"Don't," Amii begged; her body in tremors.

"A little girl!"—Miraculum shouted.

"No." Amii shook her head 'no', squeezing her eyes tight, fisting her hands.

"Once upon a time," spoke Miraculum red-faced, sweating, spittle spraying upon his lips; his eyes full of worry and fire. "Once upon a time, there was a little girl!"

"Stop this!" Amii pleaded as her eyes welled up wet; a tear dropped out of her right eye to roll in a hot streak down her cheek.

"There was a little girl!" Miraculum hollered this directly in her shuddering face, with his own eyes swelling up hot-red and wet. "The little girl was sexually abused! And she went into a seizure! And her soul split apart! But when her soul came back together, she ran into the *bathroom*!"

"Stop! *Stop*!"—cried Amii—"I don't want to talk about this!"

"And what happened Amii? What happened in that bathroom, Amii?!" Miraculum was screaming his words, his face up to hers. His eyes filled up moist; teardrops rolled over his eyelashes, poured down his cheeks. "What happened in that bathroom, Amii!?"

All at once it was as if a long lost thought, dusty from being hidden beneath some forgotten spot, a sliding piece of a puzzle suddenly dusted off it's cobwebs in a ray of shocking light. A perfectly shaped puzzle piece to a fully completed jig-saw, complete but for that one perfect missing piece now come out huge in size and flying toward her! The puzzle piece swirling, smashing, straight through Amii's head, thrusting her into dizziness. Then is a flash of bright shine Amii's ears began to ring in a shrill unpleasant sound that pierced her ears and into her consciousness. Then alas nothing at all save but blinding light; only for a moment, before it faded away like backward fog. Amii found that she was back in that bathroom from long ago. The office she had been previously standing in completely gone! In the flashback Amii saw herself as the tiny little child, while at the same time she was also in her adult body standing there watching it all take place. Reliving the moment as if it were actually taking place right then and there.

The very young little child Amii had closed and locked the bathroom door, then walked over to the toilet, kneeling in front of it, folding her palms together in prayer. Placing her little elbows on the toilet lid as if it were a church altar. Small baby-girl Amii bowing her head, eyes closed, began to pray. As Amii both relived and also watched the memory replay, she remembered something important once long tucked away hidden. She *finally* remembered the *prayer* she had so desperately prayed! "Dear God, Sweet God, I believe in you with all my heart and soul. And if you made the Angels then you also made the Demons. And if you see fit, Dear God, Oh God, I beg of you, I beg you, beg you, beg you! To please, please, please," and the little child-Amii raised her eyes and hands upwards, "please avenge me!" She lowered her small head, closing her eyes, placed her palms back in prayer, quickly continuing: "So please, send your strongest, biggest, mightiest

Demon. If you see fit." Her head snapped in the same direction as her arm out-stretched so that she pointed at the closed bathroom door saying: "*And kill that Pig!*"

After this next moment she quickly bowed her head back down, closed her eyes while placing her palms together once more in reverent prayer; little child Amii crossed herself, then kissed the fingers she'd crossed herself with, placing these kissed fingertips on her forehead. She said, "Amen."

Nauseating wave of dizziness overwhelming little child Amii; then she looked about the small dirty bathroom wondering *what* she was doing. The watching adult Amii realized that dizzy wash was the moment little child-Amii had pushed the frightening prayer she'd made, far back into the reserved forgetting oubliette in her brain. Oh; how she remembered the prayer *now*. Recalled it perfectly.

Little child-Amii walked sad of heart and soul over to the bathroom door when a bright and beautiful shining light full of flooding unconditional love beamingly gleamed, huge, gorgeous, to the right of her. From within the light she saw a glittering, miraculous face, full of kindness. Then an arm sheening with brilliance came forth from the light; cupping a large hand upward until his fingers were under her child-size chin. The glowing fingers of divine beauty lifted her chin up; the voice strong, gentle; deeply pretty, saying: "Well, you're a young one."

Adult Amii watching, repeated the words out-loud as the memory replayed, 'Well, you're a young one.' Amii next saying out loud as a tear fell, a solemn smile crossing her mouth, speaking of the melodious beautiful moment in the memory: "I thought you were an Angel." Another feverous salty teardrop tumbled down her skin.

Miraculum's deep lyrical voice floated loudly sweet into her flashback as he said, "*I thought you were one of my Brethren.*"

Amii lifted her face toward the sound of his voice; raising an arm to shield her squinting eyes from the clambering light. Shrill ringing painfully pierced her ears again; then the sound faded away as the memory's clouds disappeared. Flashback over with; gone. She licked a mineral tasting tear from the corner of her mouth while glancing at Miraculum; standing as before in her office. A few seconds of extreme quiet passed whilst Miraculum wiped streaming tears off his face; drying his eyes with his hands.

Instantly a tall rectangular door opened; Nnema walked out of it with the door vanishing behind him. Nnema had a concerned look waxing pale across his face; a slight smile attempted at his pressed lips. He was belied by the wringing of his hands together in a tight crunch. Amii gazed in shock; flung out vocally without even thinking about it: "Nnema?!"

Miraculum jerked his head in Amii's direction, brusquely soliciting: "How do *you* know his name?"

Still clammy at the sight of Nnema; feeling excruciatingly flabbergasted, Amii stuttered: "I… I've seen… seen him. In… in my dreams. Sometimes." Swaying just a tad, the disbelief rocking her that Nnema of nocturnal dreams stood real, truly solid, like any actual person despite his wizardly garb and appearance. "Oh help;" beseeched Amii, "Oh help me, help me. I'm having an hallucination!" She thought she was going to be sick.

Miraculum grasped hold of her shoulders so she was forced to face him. Specifically Miraculum willed his voice to a kind, gentle, firmness. Exploring dearly into her aged brown eyes he bravely brazened: "He's not an hallucination!" Miraculum paused for emphasis. "He's your *witness*!"

"What?" Her articulation broke weak. Color drained from her countenance. Crashing down upon Amii came the galloping rushing thought of her family and all her experiences growing up; images of her son's struggle in that haunted house. Now Nnema standing real! The weight of it all was far too much for Amii; she felt her bones and muscles quaking with waning strength. Postulated by the poverty of tottering unsteadiness. Suddenly Amii weepingly lamented: *"It's all my fault!"* *"My fault!"*—she cried out! In despair she wept ever harder so that her very shoulders shook. The cane toppled from her weakened grasp; it seemed to her that it fell in slow motion, with a loud slow-motion bouncing upon the floor. Her legs wobbled, buckled, so that Amii fell onto her knees. "I...," she began, gaping up at Miraculum, "I... called... on... *you*." Teardrops falling no more as her eyes inexplicably began drying up as if to say there were no more tears left in all the universe, for the weeping had reached it's zenith. Circling wavering loss of strength seeped the energy from every inch of her. While her head swung slowly, her vision blurred. (The words: '*I called on you*'; echoed around her unforgiving.) Amii fainted! Miraculum swiftly bent to catch her from the fall with one strong hand thrust to press her upper-back. He eased her close so she was swaddled in his arm. Then he slid his other arm beneath her legs, pulling her up to his chest, cradling her. Standing to his feet with Amii in his arms. Miraculum wrapped Amii in his caressing swaddle. She began to regain consciousness, seeing manifest his downcast tender eyes. "Now," spoke Miraculum to Amii, "Now you must do what I had to do. You must do something for yourself, that I had to do for myself."

Gathering audience from the matrimonial spell of an expression he conjured at her, she bestowed her mind's questions although her body was still weak; her voice whisper weary. "What?"—Amii questioned, "What! What must I do?"

Sharing his gaze with her: "You know what." Miraculum kissed her forehead affectionately. "You must forgive yourself." He hugged her in his warm arms and carried her. Nnema, whom had spoke not a word, walked fretfully following them. Doctor Amii Roberts had transformed her living room into her office with Japanese partitions separating, hiding, both the living room and the open kitchen. Another smaller partition just past the bathroom door closed off the hallway leading to the rest of her New York City apartment. She enacted as her own secretary which she found more aesthetically pleasing as it saved her money; and she gave so many people low-cost treatment since her sensitive tender heart ached for them. Nnema pushed the partition beside the bathroom aside for them to pass. Miraculum carried Amii, cradling her lovingly in his arms down the dark wood hallway that had pictures of her son Elijah hung to cover the walls. Elijah at age five holding a baseball bat, wearing his team uniform. Elijah at age eight smiling on top of the back of a cream-colored horse with a straw hat on his head. Elijah her precious son at birth; with his friends at camp; holding trophies; in a dapper suit with his first girlfriend whom wore a flower pinned on her yellow dress just before the boy took her off for the junior prom. There, in a crystal covered frame, stood Elijah in graduation cap and gown. The secrets of her hearts joy hung in frames hidden by a small elegant Japanese partition.

Tenderly, lovingly carrying Amii with Nnema following silently. Softly Miraculum cooed, "I'm so sorry Amii. I'm sorry for everything I ever did to you or your family."

Far too meek in her fatigued state to speak with much volume Amii raised her head a little, muttering, "You're apologizing?"

"Yes." Miraculum was sincere. Surprised, Amii merely blinked at him; her strength seeming to drowsily return. "Forgive me Amii," Miraculum daintily rumbled genuinely.

"You're asking my forgiveness?"

"Yes." It was heartfelt.

Amii cupped the palm of her chilled hand upon his warm inviting cheek. Miraculum leaned his head into her touch. "I forgive you." She spoke softly, feeling her heart pounding with an aching hurting pang mixed with all her soul's deepest love, "Are you… good now?"

Miraculum chuckled in his throat, smiling sweetly, and speaking with all truthful sincerity said, "No. I never will be. But everything's going to be alright."

"Alright?" She searched his soul for understanding.

Miraculum choked on a throb in his throat, his head bent despairingly for a second. "Amii. Don't you *get*… that I love you." Against his will tears welled up along his eyelashes, spilling over in drops.

Amii petting his cheek knew the love of which his genteel ministry sanctioned prophetically sapid. A heady spirituous brio of wafting energy flushed within and around them both. Her heart felt it would split in two for such joy and such sorrow shattering resplendent in her bosom. Miraculum and Amii both felt the wild soaring bright shimmer brilliant dementia

moon pulling it's sad comic tide
sparkling in the quickening blood,
forgiving two worlds fleeting vibration
passing, past, one another. Pale luster
moon, demagnetized of light and fog,
losing demesne to the demagoguery
magicking benevolent misery into
ponderous illuminated beauty.

Rubbing his cheek with her quivering
palm; Miraculum bending into the touch.
"I love you too, Miraculum. Since the
very first day when I thought you were
an Angel." Unbearable yet endurable,
admissible insufferable glorious hope;
feeling monstrous loneliness; soul-scars;
unimaginable loss; bonded yearning of
love's longing.

Nnema halted behind in waiting while
Miraculum bumped open Amii's
bedroom door with his elbow ever so
elegantly so as not to even slightly scathe
a hair on Amii's head. Nnema followed
Miraculum cradling Amii in his able
arms into the bedroom with the crystal

sun-catchers hanging from the window. Crystals which would have spread rainbows glittering across the room if Amii hadn't closed the curtains for darkness to take an early morning nap. All around her four-poster wrought-iron bed hung long sheer purple and white curtains with pink sashes of see-through cloth draped at the top, head, and foot of the poster-bars. Nnema parted purple white curtains hanging to the ground across the side of the bed. White fake fur covered the mattress, same white 'fur' on all pillows. Miraculum lay Amii down upon the white furry fluff where her pure white long hair flowed, splayed, sleeking around her shoulders. Nnema crossed Amii's arms so that her hands lay on top of one another above her heart. Nnema stepped, backing away. Miraculum gazed down at her. With profound certainty Amii knew, she just *knew*, what she must do. Looking up at the white gauze-like canopy sheltering the roof of the bed, Amii serenely spoke over and over again: "I forgive myself for everything I have ever done. I forgive myself for everything I have done."

When she had said it many times a cloud of sadness floated out of her heart. Love remained to be replaced by resignation's realization that she *must* live her life out after all. Amii's head rolled toward the elongated white curtains parted at the wide side of her bed to see Miraculum smiling dearly with love in his eyes; he began walking backwards into a miraculously divine sight more radiant than one could ever imagine. Dusting powdery sprinkles of multicolored light sparks twinkled amidst a brilliant white and golden light wide at the bottom, which seemed to touch the floor, streaming thus cylindrically smaller towards the top that appeared to flow up through the ceiling into the beyond. Miraculum backed into this light sparkling effervescent splendor which he felt throughout every cell,

atom, emotion, consciousness, of his
entire being. His soul proffered a
bubbling tingling after-effect like being
softly, lightly, mildly struck by
lightening. Joy filled blessed in
Miraculum with growing pleasurable
exuberance. Broiling over in excitement
as he became fully encompassed,
enveloped, in the streaming caliber
expanding juxtapose kindle light around
him. Miraculum flung upward his arms,
eyes too, soaking in a feeling within and
around him of purest powerful
unconditional love! Far up at the end of
this lighted tunnel Miraculum saw his
friends, his *family*. There was Grolin!
And Thaddeus! Tobias, Ramley, Barlee,
all the others beckoning to him; cheering
him onward and upward. Miraculum
could hardly wait to get back Home to
his Heaven and chop off Barlee's arm,
which had happened several times
already, so much it was becoming a bit of
a running gag! Yet for all friends
unsuspecting the greatest fun of all, more

deliciously exciting, would be the surprise Barlee had planned to pull on them all just to get back at them! How they all would laugh!

"HA!"—Miraculum whooped for joy! "Amii!" (She looked into his face surrounded by energies shining force.) "Goodbye forever." Peering up, exuded exhilaration filled Miraculum as he felt himself light, his weight being lifted! Quills barbuled his back, the epidermal hamuli projected petesthai in a windfall POOF of feathery plumes; he had his wings once more! Flapping his wings in one huge whooshing span, Miraculum rose upward into the light. Finally, Miraculum went Home.

Amii saw Miraculum ascend into the indescribable light, disappearing. The light vanished as if pulled back into the void. Turning her eyes unto Nnema she smiled; he returned the smile. The wizardly gentleman placed his palms together then bowed to her. Turning

around to face away from her Nnema
entered the tall rectangular shining-light
door that appeared then evaporated
instantly. The kindly fellow wearing the
garb of a wise sage; the silent witness,
was gone.

Now the room fell very dark
excepting the glimmering purple, pink,
and white night-light shaped like an
angel which Amii kept turned on
continuously that was plugged into the
wall outlet. All at once Amii felt a
presence! Glancing down she saw her
precious calico cat. The poor feline's
eyes were frightened into huge wide
saucers bigger than Amii had ever seen
them. The sleek old cat's tail was
straight up in the air, all pinged fur across
it's tail, back, and neck stood straight
outward electrical stiff. Poor kitty-cat
was terrified! Amii lay her chest against
the soft mattress; reaching down she
picked the cat up with both hands. With
kitty in her arms Amii rolled again onto

her back, placing her beloved calico upon her chest; rubbing it's fur, scratching behind the cat's ears and whiskers. Settling down with back-feet underneath belly, front paws stretched out upon Amii's heart. Pretty, silky, calico lowered it's eyelids into a happy set of nearly closed half-moons, seeming to smile.

Amii firmly, lovingly, placed her hands upon the living creature's shoulders; looking deep into it's eyes she said soothingly: "Be Not Afraid."

The End.

Suzanna Terrell is Author of: HEALING FROM : TRAUMA [CD #1] and [CD # 2] - - Includes Healing From Severe Post Traumatic Stress.   The Most POWERFUL Healing TECHNIQUES For: Divorce, Severe Post Traumatic Stress Disorder, Kidnapping, Rape, Abuse, Injustice, Loss of a Loved-One, Harm or Loss of a Child, and other traumatic events.

These CD's can be found at: [CD #1] www.createspace.com/2018745   [CD #2] createspace.com/2023259   And also at: www.amazon.com

Suzanna Terrell is also Author of the <u>True Story</u>:

a) "<u>COMFORT SOUP FOR THE MIND</u>"

b) "<u>HANDBOOK FOR THE DEAD</u>,

<u>THE LIVING DEAD, AND THOSE WHO OCCASSIONALLY WISHED THEY WERE DEAD</u>"

Which can be found at:
https:www.createspace.com/3393541   &
www.amazon.com

Suzanna Terrell is also Author of the novel: **"<u>MIRACULUM</u>"**
Which can be found at: createspace.com &
amazon.com

BONUS EXCERPT !

EXCERPT FROM:
"<u>RESTLESS IN PURGATORY</u>"
–A COLLECTION OF POEMS AND SHORT
STORIES WRITTEN BY:
SUZANNA TERRELL.

EXCERPT FROM:

"RESTLESS   IN PURGATORY"

Written By:

SUZANNA TERRELL.

CIRCLING THE LION

A Fable, _All_ Made Up & Written By :

Suzanna Terrell

(Written At Age 13.)

This is an Indian fable. A story once upon a time told by the native elders most likely around a fire at night. I will repeat it to you now as it might have been told around an open fire a long time ago. The elder would say, 'Gather around in a circle, that you may hear the story.'
Back then, everyone young and old, would gather for the night's stories. This was an important story the elder would tell. The Native story-teller would repeat it often, as with each Harvest

Moon, so that the children would
remember it, and pass it down
themselves one day to their own
descendants. Sometimes the
stories were purely
entertainment. Other times the
stories were both truthful
entertainment combined with
spiritual education. This is THE
Indian fable about, The Lion with
Wings!
The story goes like this:

It was said through out the tribes

Great Spirit Secret

Winged-Lion Eyes

Secret Truth,
Wisdom Zion

For those with courage to face the
Lion

The warrior spun
As the secret swells

If the warrior finds where the
Lion's heart melts

Many tried taking the Winged-
Lion it seems

Skilled power warriors with
sneaky schemes

They would put on their war-paint

Beat on their drums

Chanting prayers to there 'chosen
ones'

Each tribe felt they were better..

Than all other tribes

Thus the world sunk in sorrow
and holy-war crimes

Then one at a time...

Every tribe...

Every angle...

They made their attempt on the
Winged-Lion fable
Some ran at the Lion

Some snuck from behind

Some tribes danced beside him
before pouncing his side

Each tribe were killed

Bones and bodies were strewn

Each lay sick beside the Lion,
doubting their own ruin

Now the sun always rises,
And the sun always sets

And the years will pass by
Despite any tribes crest

Those who saw bodies bones
Of warriors turned to dust
Threw stones at the Lion
Defacing him thus

The Lions face, and wings,
All were affected
Pelted by time and the tribes
war-elected

Changed by the sorrow
And warring unjust
The motionless Lion lay coated
in dust

The rumors they spread
That the Lion was Dead

Yet the Winged-Lion slumbered
thus...
Waiting instead

Listen carefully children
A long time had passed
Until all tribes had lost..
Every Oar, Every Mast

Then a child in innocence,
sweetness, and wonder,
Began Circling the Lion
Who rest in his slumber

Dancing while circling

Strewing petals and singing
The child surpassed sunrises and
sunsets
streaming

The child was drawn into the
circle with Love
Not minding the rain
Sounding thunder above

A lightening bolt flew through
the child-like power
Yet the child saw Love
And the child did not cower

Inside the circle
The child fell to her knees

She kissed the poor Winged-Lions
nose,
when he sneezed

The Lion awoke with the sneeze
and the kiss
He yawned and he stretched and
he gave a soft hiss

The child put her small hand

On the Lions sore face
She saw past all erosion
Of the Lion debased

She saw past the years of the
warriors famish

Seeing the True Face of the Lion
without damage

A miracle happened
After eons of waiting
The Lion opened eyes,
Un-abating

Forced to see her True Self in the
Lions Eyes Reflection
The child looked without fear
Full of honest affection

The child looked with Love
Not fearing to die
So Love was the Reflection
Seen in the
Winged-Lions Eyes

In the heart of the child
The Winged-Lion saw

Thus *Into* the Lions Eyes
the child was drawn

Consumed not by the Lions
mouth
But by its Eyes

This child took flight
With the Lion so wise

Rising Renewed the Winged-Lion
took flight

In majestic ascent from its torrid
earth plight

Set Free the Winged-Lion
Set Free the child too

In Eyes, the Reflection of Love is
the Truth.

Carefree flights, Moonlights New
Wings abreast the Spirit True
--Reflection without Dying

Warring warriors could not do
What a little child could do

--Circling The Lion

COMFORT IN THE BLACK

Written By : **Suzanna Terrell**

(Written At Age 11.)

HIDING IN A DAMP DARK BOX

WHERE EVIL COMFORT LIE

I'D DROWN MYSELF WITH
FANTASIES

THEN BOW MY HEAD TO CRY

THE SKY IS BLACK!

THE SCENT OF SALTY TEAR-
DUST CLOUDS

CAPTURED BY THE
NIGHTMARES MASK!

ENVELOPED IN IT'S SHROUD.

SOON THE SMOOTH
FORMALDEHYDE

SHOT UP MY SPINE AND DOWN
MY BACK

IT BLURRED MY EYES, AND
THAT'S WHEN I

FOUND COMFORT IN THE
BLACK.

AT LAST SET BACK

ALL HOPE WAS GONE

BETWIXED MY MINDS DESPAIR

HELLS DREAMS INFEST
REALITIES

MY SOUL NO LONGER CARED.

THE PUPPET

Written By :

Suzanna Terrell

(Written At Age 10.)

At first you took good care of me
My very steps you did adore
And what a fine, rare, wood you
found -
Washed upon the shore.
The wood was pine with cedar
scent,
A maidens red-wood cheeks.
     Not a scar to ruin it
     Nor a tears disrupting streak
Fairies pine-dust sprinkled
Into such child-like eyes
It's magic dared the strongest oak
--- Ever to up-rise

--- The Puppet in the Making ---

You took away the cedar scent,
and what foul thing did replace!
Banish'ed the innocent red -
    Worldly wise, to stain the face
Remold me to your fancy!
    Change me with your eyes
Thicken the blood within my
veins
And turn it into ice!

Chisel away the sacred soul
Chisel to fit your favorite mold
Chisel away what pride was there-
Throw it 'neath the attic chair

--- The Puppet is Created ---

At last! The face is painted on
A smile so cold and fake
The mind confused will turn to
you...
Oh, what a grave mistake.
The elder-elders with their

Age'ed wrinkle-brows.
Bend awkwardly, to stare at me,
And Gossip,
>   Gossip down.

-- The Puppet Begins To Break --

A storm of lightening
Fierce and Bray
Came crashing through the clouds
The sky as black as evils prey
With thunders winding sounds

Droplets, droplets
Heaven's tears
Fell in the puppets eye
She raised her weary, wooden
shell
And looked into the sky
The rain fell hard against her
face
It pounded off the paint
Floating from the Rainbows sky
She clearly saw a Saint
Aroma sweet of cedar scent

The old is done away
Relief at last forever hers
To win the light of day

The strings once held, are broke
In Length
Thus gained from pain.....
     Sympathetic Strength?

--- The Puppet is Set Free ---

EARTHBOUND SPIRITS

Written By : **Suzanna Terrell** (Written At Age 7.)

Voices in the Silence
Like whispers in the trees
Screaming at each other
No-one hears them
No-one sees

Huddled in the silence
A Shroud upon their Head
Voices in the silence
Of The Sad Ones
Of The Dead.

www.ingramcontent.com/pod-product-compliance
Lightning Source LLC
Chambersburg PA
CBHW051528280626
47161CB00021B/50